THE CROOKED STRAIGHT

A mysterious series of factory and warehouse fires was creating havoc, and the police did not appear to be getting on the track. So the *Globe* newspaper hired private eye Nat Craig to see what he could discover. Craig's investigations lead him to suspect arson as part of an insurance fraud, but when two young women are found brutally murdered he soon realises that the arson and murders may be connected. But who is the mastermind behind it all?

ERNEST DUDLEY

THE CROOKED STRAIGHT

Complete and Unabridged

LINFORD
Leicester

First published in Great Britain

First Linford Edition
published 2007

British Library CIP Data

Dudley, Ernest
  The crooked straight.—Large print ed.—
Linford mystery library
  1. Private investigators—Fiction
  2. Murder—Investigation—Fiction
  3. Detective and mystery stories
  4. Large type books
  I. Title
  823.9'12 [F]

  ISBN 978–1–84617–833–7

Published by
F. A. Thorpe (Publishing)
Anstey, Leicestershire

Set by Words & Graphics Ltd.
Anstey, Leicestershire
Printed and bound in Great Britain by
T. J. International Ltd., Padstow, Cornwall

This book is printed on acid-free paper

'Dreamer of dreams, born out of my
  due time,
Why should I strive to set the crooked
  straight?'

WILLIAM MORRIS

1

'I've been taking a little look round,' Hillman said. 'I get the impression this town is full of rackets.'

Sullivan, his managing editor, grinned sardonically:

'You don't say?'

'All kinds of things are going on,' Hillman continued. 'Kinds of things the readers of the *Globe* ought to know about.'

Sullivan raised a quizzical eyebrow at Hillman and then he helped himself from the ornate cigarette-box. The managing editor was on those sort of terms with his boss. He eyed Hillman curiously over the flame of his lighter. He was wondering what sort of bee was buzzing in his bonnet now.

'I'll tell you where I would start,' Hillman said. 'There was a fire down in the East End last night. Shoreditch. Factory where they made paper-bags and cartons, though it went out of business a month ago.'

The proprietor of the *Globe* paused, then he leaned across his desk and jabbed a well-manicured finger at Sullivan. 'Who owns the place? Where was it insured?'

'Search me.'

'Maybe we should find it was insured three or four times over with different companies. Maybe we should find it was owned by the same bunch who owned the hotel at Richmond which happened to burn itself out six weeks ago.'

'You mean, you're suggesting the Shoreditch fire was fixed?'

'It would be worth looking into. I've been checking through our files. In the past six months there have been at least three other fires. Two warehouses and a factory.' He paused again and added: 'I just think it's a possibility that might yield some pretty readable material.'

'Bit far-fetched,' Sullivan said. 'In any case, I've got a man covering the Press Bureau at Scotland Yard — '

'The Press Bureau!' Hillman laughed shortly. 'The stuff they hand out wouldn't

2

make the back page of a Sunday school magazine. It isn't news. It's history.'

The managing editor shrugged. He was trying to work out in his mind what the boss was leading up to. He said, tentatively:

'I still don't think there's all that in it.'

'I was thinking,' the other went on relentlessly, 'it might be a nice stunt to hire our own private eye.'

Sullivan looked at him questioningly.

'Private dick — detective,' the other explained slightly irritably. He went on: 'It would be nice if we could show up Scotland Yard on this stuff.'

'Very nice,' Sullivan said drily. 'If you could. A newspaper running its own private detective agency is certainly something new.'

'What's so funny about it?'

'To start with, there isn't anyone in this town any better than a cheap keyhole-peeper. Divorce racket is about all most private detectives work at here.'

'That may be true about some of 'em,' Hillman said judiciously. 'But there's one I know of who's done some pretty smart jobs. Blackmail, insurance company swindles. Even murder. Matter of fact, he doesn't touch divorce.'

'Who is he?'

'His name's Craig.'

2

I

It was six o'clock. The girl typists had all left. Behind a frosted-glass door, in his nicely furnished office, a man sat at a wide desk reading a letter. He frowned as he got up and locked the letter in his safe.

He lit a cigarette and drew at it nervously. He glanced at his watch and paced up and down the room. Suddenly the switchboard in the outer office buzzed. He went out and plugged the line through to his 'phone, then he went back and lifted the receiver.

'Yes? Speaking.'

He listened while the voice at the other end began to give instructions. Then he interrupted:

'Look. I think we should postpone it. One of the girls here has found out something. She's going to be difficult. Yes, I know. It's damn serious. What? She lives at number five, Vale Crescent, Maida Vale. You'd better leave her to me. I don't want to do anything in a hurry. I want to think this thing out. Will you 'phone me later? At my club. Trust me, I'll be careful.'

He cradled the receiver and began humming a little tune to himself.

II

At a quarter past six Gabriel Warwick walked out of the offices of Pyramid Assurance. The commissionaire saluted him and raised his hand for a taxi.

As Warwick stood waiting, he drew a gold watch from his waistcoat pocket. A glance at it reassured him. He had plenty of time to get to the Café Rouge. He made quite an elegant and impressive personality, which, being the managing-director of Pyramid Assurance, was the way it should be. He wore chamois leather gloves and carried a heavy silver-topped walking-stick.

He was a little worried about what he

was going to say to the shareholders at the general meeting next day. There had been a somewhat unusual number of heavy fire claims paid out in the past year and he would have to assure the shareholders that Pyramid's assessors were completely satisfied these claims were legitimate. He knew, as a matter of fact, they were far from satisfied. It had been an unsatisfactory financial year one way and another, and Gabriel Warwick didn't like it.

He sighed. The shareholders' meeting was to be in the afternoon. In the morning he had promised to put in an appearance at the wedding of Jeffrey Brook. He was on his way now to have a drink with Brook and the girl who was to be his wife.

The commissionaire stepped forward and opened the door of the taxi. Gabriel Warwick was about to get in when another man came out of the Pyramid offices.

Gabriel Warwick turned to him.

'Hello, Brook. I thought you'd already gone. Hop in and we'll go along together.'

The other appeared momentarily startled, but he quickly pulled himself together.

'Thank you.'

'Your last few hours of freedom,' observed Gabriel Warwick jocularly. He chuckled as the other started. 'The bridegroom usually spends the night before his wedding having grave doubts, so I'm told. However, perhaps a large drink will cheer you up.'

III

The Café Rouge was crowded.

'Your pal doesn't appear to be here,' Nat Craig said. 'Let's go home. I never liked getting mixed up with weddings anyway.'

Simone threw him a veiled glance, but Craig wasn't looking at her.

'There she is, over there,' Simone said and led the way to a corner table.

Helen March had warm brown eyes which gave the impression of being affectionate and trusting. With her were two men. She introduced them as Jeffrey

Brook and Gabriel Warwick, and Simone explained to Craig which one her friend was going to marry next day. Craig didn't need to be told. It was obvious enough the way Helen March kept looking at Brook.

Jeffrey Brook had one of those firm jaws, plus a somewhat concentrated expression, which was inclined to make him look slightly savage. Craig decided he was a very determined chap. He thought, too, he sensed an attitude about him that was slightly disconcerting. It was as if Jeffrey Brook were always watching and waiting.

'Let's drink to the happy couple.'

It was Gabriel Warwick who was lifting his glass. Craig turned his attention to him. He was obviously in a jovial mood. Craig pigeon-holed him mentally as a successful business man with shrewdness and acumen plus underlying his jocularity.

Jeffrey Brook's set face relaxed in a self-conscious smile. He suddenly looked very much younger, almost boyish. His smile grew warm and tender as he looked over his glass at Helen March.

Simone chuckled and said, in her husky French accent:

'May all your troubles be little ones.'

'You should try being original,' Craig told her. 'You're getting to be quite a big girl now.'

She pulled a face at him and they drank.

Putting down his glass Jeffrey Brook looked uneasily round, then said apologetically:

'There's a 'phone-call I have to make. If you will excuse me for a moment.'

As he went off Gabriel Warwick pulled out his watch and said:

'I'll be getting along, too.'

'The party's breaking up,' Simone grumbled.

'Wait until Jeff comes back, Mr. Warwick,' Helen said.

Gabriel Warwick had turned a speculative glance on Craig. 'I was thinking,' he began slowly. 'Mr. Craig, would you be interested in handling a job for my firm? Pyramid Assurance. We've been having a lot of fire claims. Too many, in fact. I was

10

wondering if — '

He broke off as if waiting for Craig's reaction.

Craig grinned across at him and said:

'This makes the second job I've been offered to-day. The other's about some fires, too.'

3

Gabriel Warwick regarded Craig, a glint of amusement in his eyes.

'Nice to be in demand.'

'We are very good detectives,' Simone said. 'Did not anyone tell you?'

'We?'

'I am Mr. Craig's secretary.'

Gabriel Warwick nodded, his expression perfectly serious. 'That explains,' he said.

Simone flashed him a smile. He smiled back broadly at her, then turned to Craig.

'Would it be a leading question if I asked you who the other people are who're also having fire trouble?'

Craig said:

'I always make it a rule to answer leading questions. Not always strictly accurately, naturally. I'm hired by the *Globe*. It's a kind of gag they're working.'

'You mean your job's to find out if there's anything — er — funny behind these fires?'

Craig nodded.

'And they have your services exclusively?' the other asked.

Craig said, through a cloud of cigarette-smoke:

'Why not put it into words? You want me to go to work for you. Maybe I could handle it. But the fact that I'd be covering the same ground for someone else won't scale down my fee.'

Gabriel Warwick laughed good-humouredly.

'We might do a deal, then. Ring my office in the morning. My secretary will fix an appointment and we'll go into the whole thing.'

Gabriel Warwick had gone when Jeffrey Brook rejoined them. His face was clouded and he gave Helen March an apologetic glance. He said with a casualness that was a shade over-elaborate:

'Afraid I'll have to leave you. I have to see a man. It's rather important.'

'Oh, Jeff,' the girl said with a little gasp.

'I'm very sorry to have to go like this. It's a big deal I've been trying to tie up for weeks and I have a chance of seeing the man to-night before he goes away.'

Craig was looking at Helen March. He had surprised an odd expression in her eyes as she stared up at Jeffrey Brook. She'd gone suddenly pale and bit her lower lip nervously. It was just a momentary change, then she sat back, her eyes shadowed. Craig wondered why young Brook's business appointment should affect her so strangely. It almost looked as if she were frightened of something.

Simone gave Craig a look and, leaning across, said to her:

'Mr. Craig could ask you to come round to his place for a drink. If the boy-friend gets through with his business soon, he can pick you up there.'

The girl turned to Craig and he grinned back at her.

'I — I'd love to,' she said.

'Fine,' Craig told her.

Jeffrey Brook said he expected he'd be through in an hour. Outside the Café Rouge he left them and went off in the direction of Piccadilly Circus.

Craig noticed that the girl seemed

uneasy as the three of them got into a taxi. By the time they'd arrived at his flat, which was also his office, she had responded somewhat to Simone's efforts to add a little gaiety to the conversation.

'Don't look so depressed, darling,' she told the other as she took a drink from Craig and gave it to her. 'If you're worrying about him leaving you like that, let me tell you you should be grateful for picking a husband who doesn't mind going to work.'

'I know,' Helen admitted. 'You see, he's just taken over a new job at the office and he's giving all his time to it just now.'

Craig lit a cigarette for her while Simone encouraged Helen to talk about herself and to-morrow's wedding. Craig watched her speculatively over his drink. It was no business of his, but he couldn't help being idly curious about her and what it was that was frightening her.

It was after eight o'clock when the telephone rang.

'*Globe*,' the voice over the wire told Craig. 'News editor wants you.'

The news editor came on the line.

'Craig? Sorry to disturb you.'

'Where's the fire?'

The news editor's laugh rattled Craig's ear-drum.

'No fire. But there's another little job which we thought might interest you.' He coughed and added: 'Since you're on our pay-roll and all that.'

There was a pause which Craig was expected to fill in, but he didn't say a thing.

The news editor coughed again apologetically.

'As it happens, there's no one in the office just now. I'll send a reporter down after you as soon as I can. It's number 5, Vale Crescent, Maida Vale.'

'What's at number 5, Vale Crescent, Maida Vale?'

'A girl. She's been found murdered.'

4

There was a police car drawn up outside number five and Craig's taxi stopped just behind it. As Craig got out, he spotted among the people outside the house several newspapermen whom he knew. He made his way casually over to one of them.

'Who's running the show to-night?' He nodded towards the house.

'Marraby,' replied the other, giving Craig a curious look. 'What are you doing here? Is there anything in this for you?'

'Could be.'

'He won't let you in,' the newspaperman called after him bitterly. 'Won't let anyone in. Gratitude, that is. After that donation I made to the police sports.'

Craig knew Detective Inspector Marraby all right. It was going to be a tough job getting into the house. He walked slowly to the corner of the terrace and found a mews which ran along the back.

He counted the dark four-storey houses until he came to the back door of number five. The door of the basement was unlocked and he made his way into the kitchen.

The light was on, but nobody was about. Something was sizzling on the gas-stove and there was a strong smell of burning. Craig moved into a dim passage and found the stairs. The smell of burning followed him as he went on up. On the ground floor a policeman was shepherding people into one of the rooms. Craig glimpsed two girls in dressing-gowns, another in street clothes, a frowsy, unshaven man and another woman who looked like his wife. There was also a sour-faced woman who was making threatening remarks to the policeman and seemed to be the landlady.

Craig went on up swiftly and quietly. He heard voices from the second room along the landing. It was a bed-sitting-room, with faded yellow wallpaper and yellowish curtains. A divan bed covered with chintz, an armchair, a cheap painted wardrobe, a small table and a gas-ring completed the furniture. Leaning unobtrusively in the doorway, Craig took in the scene.

The police surgeon was bending over the dead girl. She was a blonde, with what had once been a pretty pouting mouth. The eyes were open, but only the whites showed, making her face a grotesque mask. Her neck was discoloured and bruised. It looked as if she had been strangled.

Craig shifted his gaze to Inspector Marraby, a large, burly character with heavy brows. He wore a dark overcoat and a perpetually aggrieved expression. He looked up as Craig eased himself into the room.

'I see we're working together again,' Craig said.

'Who the hell let you in?' Marraby demanded, glowering at him from under his thick eyebrows.

'I kind of pioneered my way.'

A younger plain-clothes sergeant came forward belligerently.

'Excuse me,' he asked coldly, 'but who are you?'

Craig smiled at him agreeably. He

knew he would have to watch his step if he wanted to stick around. Although he was on good terms with Marraby, that still wouldn't prevent him from being thrown out on his ear unless he could put in some fast thinking.

'All right,' Marraby told the sergeant. Then to Craig: 'You'll have to go. I don't know what you want here anyway, but I'm talking to the newspaper boys presently. I'll see you then.'

Craig said, casually:

'Haven't you heard, Inspector? I'm working for the *Globe* nowadays. Special assignment. You know the stuff. Idea is I'm going to show Scotland Yard how to clean up crime.'

He laughed as if it were quite a joke.

The sergeant started to say something, but Craig went on imperturbably:

'But, seeing we're old pals, maybe I could do you a good turn and see you get all the credit. After all, you deserve it and I'd be glad for you to get it.'

He tried to sound as ingratiating as he could, but Marraby's eye was coldly disbelieving.

'Kind of you, only I don't need building up,' he said heavily. 'You'll oblige me by getting outside and staying outside.'

Craig shrugged and silently prayed for a miracle to save the situation. There was a sudden commotion outside and the thin-lipped woman he'd seen downstairs and guessed was the landlady pushed her way into the room. She was trying to shake off the grip of the same policeman he'd heard her threatening.

'I don't know what the police are coming to,' she declared stridently. 'Trying to stop a respectable woman from demanding her rights.'

Inspector Marraby regarded her with acute disfavour.

'What's the matter?'

'And I won't stand no nonsense from you,' the woman sailed in to the attack. 'Just because you're an inspector or something, instead of an ordinary copper, you think you can come the high and mighty with me. Letting this man here push me about as if I were an escaped convict or something.'

'Now, don't get excited. He's not pushing you about. He's just trying to keep the place clear while we make our routine examination. If you'll do as you're asked, I'm sure there won't be any trouble.' He turned to the sergeant: 'Take this lady downstairs and if there's anything she wants to tell you, listen to what she has to say.'

The sergeant nodded and moved towards the woman, but she waved him off.

'Don't you dare touch me.'

'Now, come along — '

'I'll do no such thing. I'm going to settle this here and now. A fine thing if a lady can't have her say where and when she likes in her own house.'

She hitched up the shoulder of her dress which had been pulled awry during her struggle with the policeman and prepared to plunge into her speech. It was then Craig saw his chance. He stepped outside the room and sniffed loudly.

'Seems to be something burning,' he said over his shoulder.

The smell of something burning drifted

into the room and caught the woman's nostrils.

'My dinner!' she yelled. 'Gawdalmighty, my dinner!' and she shot out.

Craig glanced at Marraby with a triumphant grin and followed the woman downstairs. If he could contrive to pacify her, he would earn the Inspector's gratitude and that ought to clinch his being allowed to stick around. He followed the landlady into the kitchen.

'This is the last straw,' she was choking as she stood over the smoking gas-stove. 'This is more than I can stand.'

Her gaze rested on Craig. She was about to burst forth with a stream of indignation, but he got in before she could get going.

'You have my sincerest sympathy,' he told her understandingly. 'A good meal ruined and all on account of those dumb-bells upstairs. Too bad. Too bad.'

He shook his head sadly.

'I'll have damages for this,' she said. 'I'll sue them.'

'It's about time these cops were told where they get off,' Craig agreed smoothly.

'I'm going to write this up — '

'You a newspaperman?'

'You're a smart girl,' he grinned at her admiringly. 'That's right. The *Globe*.'

'I take the *Globe*,' she said.

'I thought you looked the intellectual type,' he said without a hint of sarcasm. He went on: 'I'm going to write this up. All about you. I'll expose those flatties upstairs and tell the world what they did to you. We're going to have some justice around here.'

He became so vehement he almost began to believe it himself. The woman lapped up every word of it and presently she was answering his questions without the slightest suspicion of his ulterior motives. It was easier than taking sweets from a baby.

The name of the murdered girl, it appeared, was Lucy Evans. She was aged about twenty-seven. A nice girl, but a bit apt, the woman said, to get behind with the rent.

'What was her job?'

'She was a secretary in an office. Somewhere near Victoria. I never knew the name of the place, but I've got her 'phone number. She always said if anyone 'phoned her here, I was to put them on to the office.' She shuddered slightly. 'Makes me feel quite queer now I'm just beginning to realise she's dead. Those cops upstairs upset me so much, I didn't have time to think about it before.'

Craig gave a sympathetic nod.

'You were saying you had her 'phone number?'

She took a grubby exercise book from the dresser and thumbed the pages.

'Here it is. 'Victoria 5170'.'

Craig made a note of it on the back of an envelope. As he was slipping it into his pocket he noticed a photograph on the mantelpiece. It was of the blonde upstairs. It was signed: 'With love, Lucy.'

The woman followed his eye.

'That's her.'

'She looks the sort who might have had one or two boy-friends,' he suggested.

'She did have one gentleman friend,' the other replied with a primness that was almost obscene. 'She might have had more. I'm not nosey. Keep meself to

25

meself. Love and let love, that's my motto.'

Craig obliged with a smile at her heavy witticism. She went on:

'There's a separate bell for each room outside the front door. If any of my tenants has a visitor, their bell rings and they go down and let 'em in themselves. I don't see the visitors at all, unless I happen to. But of course I can't help knowing what's going on, to a certain extent. If you follow my meaning.'

He indicated that he followed her meaning all right.

'D'you happen to know if anyone came to see Lucy to-night?'

'Someone did come to see her to-night,' she nodded vigorously. 'Someone came and she let him in.' She shuddered convulsively. 'To think it might have been him doing her in and me down here all the time. Makes me feel all over alike, it does.'

'A man came to see Lucy this evening?'

'I tell you I never give it a thought at the time. Must have been about half-past seven when he come. Only I didn't attach any special meaning to it, you understand. As I said, it isn't unusual for my tenants to have visitors.'

'How d'you know he was dropping in on Lucy?'

She hesitated for a moment, then:

'I happened to hear her voice in the hall as she let him in.'

He regarded her thoughtfully for a moment, keeping the distaste he felt for her out of his expression.

'You didn't happen to hear him leaving, by any chance?'

She pretended to think back.

'Now I come to think of it,' she said slowly, 'I did hear someone going out. At a quarter to eight, it was. I remember the time because my clock was striking. Mind you, it might not have been him. I wasn't paying any particular attention, of course.'

'Of course.'

'But I did hear the front door open and close.'

'Then what?'

She threw him a slightly puzzled look.

'What happened after that?' he said.

'Nothink. At least not for about ten

minutes. Then Miss Duveen — she's the young lady in number seven — started screaming fit to bring the house down. I went up and there she was, throwing a fit, as you might say, in Lucy's room. As soon as I saw what was up, I telephoned the cops. Quite calm, I was. I suppose I'm used to people passing out. My old man died right here in this kitchen. Having a cup of tea, he was, at the time and he dropped off without a word. Just like that.'

Craig interrupted her reminiscing to ask:

'Just one thing more. Did Lucy Evans have any family? Any relatives?'

She shook her head.

'Couldn't tell you. I believe she once did say something about relatives up in the north somewhere. But I don't know who they were. She didn't talk much about herself. Oh,' she said suddenly, 'there were some friends at Putney she used to visit. I remember her mentioning them.'

'Did she tell you their name?'

'Name of Vickers. But I never knew

their address exactly. Just they lived at Putney, that's all. You'll let me know when you write all that in the newspaper, won't you?'

Craig reassured her and, leaving her to moan over her ruined dinner, he went back upstairs.

5

They were taking photographs of the body. The police surgeon had just finished his examination and was chatting quietly to Marraby.

'No doubt about the cause of death,' he was saying. 'Asphyxia due to manual strangulation.' He polished his pince-nez and replaced them on his nose. 'Strangling is not a woman's method of killing, so the murderer is probably a man. But of course that part of it is your pigeon.'

'What time would you put it at?'

The other pursed his lips judiciously.

'Fairly recently. Impossible to say exactly. Rigor mortis not very advanced. I'd say no more than a couple of hours ago. Probably not as long as that. How would it suit you if I fixed it between one hour and two hours ago?'

'If it suits you, suits me,' the Inspector said.

'Right.'

Marraby glanced at his watch. He mused:

'Just on nine now. According to you, she might have been done in about seven-thirty, or any time from then up to about eight-thirty. We were here just before eight-fifteen, weren't we, sergeant?'

'That's right.'

'So it must have been between seven-thirty and eight-fifteen.'

The police surgeon nodded.

'That's as near as you can make it,' he said.

Marraby turned to Craig, his face an aggressive question-mark.

'Scotland Yard should teach you how to cultivate natural charm,' Craig grinned at him affably. 'It pays off. That old trout downstairs is right under my spell. Tamed.'

The Inspector grunted noncommittally. Then, with a shrug he turned to the photographers and Craig threw a triumphant wink at the sergeant. His manoeuvre had come off. He could stick around.

Craig glanced casually around the

room, then, looking down, noticed a wastepaper basket. He saw it contained a crumpled piece of paper. Nobody was watching him as he bent quickly and picked it up. It was a letter which had been thrown away unfinished.

'*Darling, I am thinking of you always. There is no one else for me but you. Why don't you telephone? Did you get my other letter? I mean what I said, darling. If you don't stand by your promise, I shall — '*

That was all.

The address, 5, Vale Crescent, was written at the top, but there was no date. The writing was in green ink. It looked as if a woman had written it.

Craig called to Marraby:

'What d'you think of this?'

The other took the crumpled letter. His heavy brows drew together as he read it. He looked up.

'Where d'you get it?'

Craig nodded at the wastepaper basket.

'Don't touch anything else,' Marraby

growled at him. 'We haven't been over this room yet.'

Craig said:

'That's what I thought.'

The Inspector gave him a dirty look, but Craig's expression was blandly innocent. He indicated a bottle of green ink on the mantelpiece.

'Just in case you haven't already worked it out for yourself, I'd say she wrote it.'

Craig was remembering what the woman downstairs had told him about Lucy Evans' boy-friend and the visitor who called that night at seven-thirty. He offered:

'She was writing to her boy-friend. She was going to threaten him with something. That's what it looks like, doesn't it? And then he suddenly came to see her to-night. Naturally, she wouldn't want him to see the letter, so she crumpled it up and threw it away.'

'When I want a private dick to help me, I'll certainly hire you,' the Inspector said, 'but until then you can save it.' He gave Craig a quick look. 'Who did you say you were working for on this?'

'The *Globe*.'

The other sniffed.

'I always thought you were choosey about who employed you.'

Craig let it ride. He was too busy worrying the idea that was forming in his mind to enter into a discussion on ethics.

Suppose Lucy Evans had been hoping to marry this character the landlady had told him about? Supposing he'd promised he'd marry her and then she'd found out he was going to walk out on her? Yes, Craig thought, it could be. She'd written him letters. Letters like the bit she'd thrown into the wastepaper basket. 'Darling, I am thinking of you always. There is no one else for me but you. Why don't you telephone? Did you get my other letter? I mean what I said, darling. If you don't stand by your promise, I shall — '

The threat, whatever it was, was obviously a repetition of a threat in an earlier letter she'd written him. 'I mean what I say. If you don't stand by your promise, I shall — '

What was it that she was threatening to do?

Something that she knew would put the man in one hell of a spot. That was what had made him come round to see her that night. In answer to her first letter, that would be, or to a 'phone-call. He had arrived just as she was writing the second letter, and she'd slung it hastily into the wastepaper-basket.

There had been a row between them. Lucy Evans had gone off the handle. The man had realised she really intended carrying out her threat. A threat that might wreck his life. With a sudden rage he had grabbed her by the throat and squeezed the life out of her. It was the sort of thing that had happened plenty of times before.

It seemed to Craig the obvious line of investigation would be to check up on the girl at her office and find out, if possible, the identity of the man she'd been going around with.

'What's this?'

It was the sergeant who held up a button he'd retrieved from just under the edge of the divan-bed.

'A button,' the sergeant said, somewhat unnecessarily. 'Moreover, a man's button. Looks as if it might have been torn from his jacket.'

Marraby took it and then handed it back.

'I would estimate,' he said, without any humour, 'that every month in the Metropolitan area about one thousand buttons come adrift from men's jackets.'

The sergeant said defensively:

'I didn't imagine for one moment it was important.'

'Come on,' the Inspector said, 'let's go down and get these statements straight.'

The sergeant followed Marraby downstairs and Craig made his way leisurely after them.

One of the girls in dressing-gowns was huddled on a chair crying. The other girl, similarly attired, and the one who was dressed for the street, eyed the detectives sulkily. They were quiet and watchful. The frowsy couple Craig took to be man and wife whispered together sibilantly.

None of them could add a thing to

what was already known. None of them had heard anything that was of any significance. They had each been in their respective rooms and nothing unusual had disturbed them. The girl who was crying stated between sobs she had heard Lucy Evans bring someone upstairs earlier in the evening. That was all.

The other girl, who revealed herself as the Miss Duveen the landlady had mentioned, described how she had gone along to Lucy's room for a match. She wanted to light a cigarette, she said, and her lighter had gone back on her. Questioned further, she remembered seeing Lucy with a man about a week previously.

What kind of a man?

Well, a fairly ordinary sort of a man, nicely dressed.

No, not old.

No, not young.

Well, about thirty.

It was about here that Craig realised there would be nothing more of interest to him. He decided to fade. Dodging the landlady, he went out the way he had come.

On the corner of Vale Crescent he slipped into a 'phone-box. Would they tell him the name of the subscriber whose number was Victoria 5170? After some delay, he got the information. The subscriber whose number was Victoria 5170 was The South London Property Development Company.

Next Craig got through to the *Globe* night editor.

'I'm sorry,' the night editor began, 'I've not been able to get a reporter down to you — '

'Think nothing of it,' Craig interrupted him. 'Is this the stuff you want? The girl was found strangled in her bed-sitting-room at 5, Vale Crescent, Maida Vale. Her name is Lucy Evans. Blonde, pretty and pert. At least she was. She worked at The South London Property Development Company, Victoria. Believed to have been bumped-off about seven-thirty, doctor's estimate, or possibly during the next half-hour or so. It's known a man visited her at seven-thirty and left at a quarter to eight. Yours truly found a half-finished letter written by Lucy, probably to her boyfriend. 'Darling, I am thinking of you always — ' (not you, this is her letter). 'Darling, I am thinking of you always. There is no one else for me but you. Why don't you telephone? Did you get my other letter? I mean what I said, darling. If you don't stand by your promise, I shall — ' That's all there was. It ended there. Any more you want to know? Or have you gone to sleep?'

The night editor said it was great stuff and if he'd hang on he'd put him on to somebody who'd take it down.

Craig quitted the 'phone-box a few minutes later and found a taxi.

Jeffrey Brook was there when he got back and Helen March was just getting ready to go. Craig's appearance was a signal for Simone to get him a drink and a battery of questions from her and Helen March. He gave only evasive replies. It wasn't until afterwards that he remembered Jeffrey Brook didn't join in with the others at all.

Simone, with a quizzical look at Craig, deftly switched the conversation. Jeffrey Brook and the girl were at the door on their way and Craig was just lighting a cigarette when he noticed a button was missing from Jeffrey Brook's coat. It looked as if it had been recently torn off. Brook didn't notice the way Craig was staring at him. Then Craig told himself not to be a fool.

It was just one of those coincidences.

6

Helen March woke up to find brilliant sunshine streaming into her room. It surprised her she had been to sleep at all. For hours during the night she had listened to the nearby church clock. But at last her over-active nerves must have yielded, for here she was, suddenly awake, and it was morning.

It was the morning she was going to be married.

It was eight o'clock by her little wrist-watch. The wedding was to be at midday. She got out of bed and went to the open window. She felt the sunshine warm on her face.

She realised now how foolish she had been to worry the way she had about Jeff. After twelve o'clock he would be hers. No longer any uncertainty then.

His increasingly strange behaviour during the past weeks had troubled her. One night when they had been going out to a theatre he had made an excuse at the last moment. Something about he had to keep an unexpected business appointment. The explanation had seemed perfectly natural, but when the same thing happened two nights later, and again the next night, it hadn't looked so good.

Jeff was always telephoning to put her off after that. In fact, during these few weeks it seemed she had hardly seen him at all.

'Darling, I have to go to a dinner party. It's business.'

He had said that to her four days ago. She had accepted the explanation as she had accepted all the others, secretly worrying and afraid. Then she had decided to take in a movie alone to help ease the problem that was nagging more and more at the back of her mind. Then, out of all the people in the wide world, she had to see Jeff in Piccadilly Circus tube station.

He was talking to a woman. A blonde who wore a cheap dress, and Helen couldn't imagine how Jeff had met up with her. The girl certainly didn't fit in with the dinner party he'd told her about.

Jeff had explained when she had at last summoned up courage enough to face him. He'd been on his way to the dinner, a little late on account of business, and had met the girl accidentally. She was a secretary in somebody's office, he had said.

There was a knock on the door. It was the daily help with a cup of tea. She was a square-shaped woman with tired eyes which saw little good in the world.

'Thought you'd like this,' she said, gazing glumly at Helen, as if she were a condemned prisoner on the morning of execution. 'Shall I bring a spot of breakfast up to you?'

Helen shook her head.

'I couldn't possibly eat anything.'

'I sympathise with you. You loses your appetite when you know you've got to give your all in the lottery of marriage.'

Helen laughed.

'Believe me, marriage is a lottery.' The other shook her head morosely. 'Has your husband got a good job? You mind you don't find all of a sudden you have to go to work for him.'

The door closed on her, but she was back presently.

'A gentleman to see you. Says his name is Mr. March.'

'Good Lord. Uncle Albert. Show him up.'

Helen scrambled into her dressing-gown, wondering why on earth Uncle Albert had to arrive at such a fantastically early hour. She sighed and gulped some tea. It was just like him.

Uncle Albert was a weather-beaten character, with wispy hair and a port-wine nose which seemed to clash violently with his bow tie. He beamed at her fatuously:

'How is the blushing bride?'

Helen groaned inwardly. Uncle Albert was inclined to be vaguely humorous after his fashion.

'A few hours from now and you'll have sold yourself into bondage, my dear,' he was chuckling. 'For better or worse, eh? But don't worry too much. You'll soon settle down. Novelty will wear off and then you'll be able to look back on this morning, wondering why it bothered you at all. I remember I was in an awful state at my wedding. That was in — let me see — '08. Or was it '09? I can't even remember the date now. Just shows.'

She smiled at him brightly.

'Yes, doesn't it.'

Helen realised it was going to be grimmer than even she had anticipated. She got rid of Uncle Albert while she dressed. When he pottered back again, still bubbling over with irrepressible good humour, it was past ten. Then it seemed she was giving herself a last look as she passed a long mirror in the hall and Uncle Albert was handing her into the taxi.

It was as if she were floating on his arm as they went into the church.

7

'*Wilt thou have this woman Helen to be thy wedded wife . . .* ' (Sometimes, when he had been late meeting her, when he had forgotten to 'phone, and that time when she had seen him at the Piccadilly Circus tube — but the droning voice drove away the chill that had suddenly gripped her heart.) ' . . . *Wilt thou love her, comfort her, honour, and keep her in sickness and in health; and, forsaking all other, keep thee only unto her, so long as ye both shall live?*'

Jeff's voice was low and clear.

'I will.'

'*Wilt thou have this man Jeffrey to be thy wedded husband . . .* ' (It was going to be all right. The long months of happy meetings, tense good-byes, anxious waitings, doubts, fears and those marvellous moments when a telephone-call could mean so much, the fears, foolish fears they must prove to be, that had made a dark shadow over her life, and that time when she had seen him at the Piccadilly Circus tube — with a tremendous effort she pulled herself together again and refused to think about it.) ' . . . *Wilt thou obey him, and serve him, love, honour, and keep him in sickness and in health; and, forsaking all other, keep thee only unto him, so long as ye both shall live?*'

'I will.'

It didn't sound like her voice at all. It was as if someone else were saying it for her.

Then her hand was being taken by Jeffrey. He began to speak quietly.

'I, Jeffrey, take thee, Helen, to be my wedded wife . . . '

And now she found herself speaking. Her voice grew more confident, more poised, more certain as she spoke the words:

'I, Helen, take thee, Jeffrey, to be my wedded husband . . . '

The ring was being placed on her finger. Jeffrey was speaking again.

'With this Ring I thee wed, with my body I thee worship, and with all my wordly goods I thee endow: In the Name of the Father, and the Son, and the Holy Ghost. Amen.'

It was Uncle Albert who bought a midday edition from a passing newsboy as he followed them into Jeffrey's car. The headlines on the front page caught Helen's eye:

STRANGLED GIRL MYSTERY
MAIDA VALE MURDER

Underneath a large picture loomed out. A blonde. Helen stared at it.

She tried to focus her eyes on the picture again. Now it stared back at her clearly, so clearly she would remember it all her life.

It was the girl she had seen with Jeffrey at Piccadilly Circus tube station.

8

Simone Thérèse Marie Antoinette Lamont put her head round the door of Craig's office.

'The Professor is here again.'

Craig eyed her over his feet, which were, as usual, propped up on his desk.

'What d'you expect me to do about it? Deal with him, will you? Just treat him gently and send him away.'

'He wants to see you.'

'Tell him I've gone to Pago-Pago and you don't know when I'll be back. Come to think of it,' he added reflectively, 'I probably never would come back once I got to Pago-Pago. I once met a man who told me it was quite a place.'

His eyes shifted to a spot over Simone's shoulder.

'Too late,' he said bitterly.

'Good morning,' the Professor greeted him eagerly, sidling from behind Simone. 'I am so glad you are able to see me. I have come to give you the most sensational idea you have ever imagined.'

The Professor, whose name was Banbury or Barlow or Barnard, or something — Craig could never remember and couldn't care less — wore dark spectacles, a dirty mackintosh and was clutching a bowler hat. His bald, dome-like brow rose from a fringe of dirty grey hair that straggled over a scurf-encrusted collar. Craig raised his eyes ceilingwards as Simone, throwing the Professor a dirty look, went out, closing the door after her.

Craig said:

'What's on your mind?'

'I have made a discovery of the utmost importance in connection with the strangling of that woman in Maida Vale.' The Professor invariably adopted a special style of circumlocution when giving his ideas to the world.

'I have been analysing this crime from a scientific point of view,' he went on, 'and suddenly I was struck by a very remarkable fact. It is a fact which is significant to me, though the ignorant layman might call it a coincidence. It fits in entirely with my theory that the Universe is a perfect entity working in cycles with mathematical precision. Did you notice the moon?'

He threw the question at Craig eagerly.

'The moon?'

'Last night, the night of the murder, the moon was full.' The Professor's eyes glinted with a curious pink glow behind his spectacles. 'The influence of the moon on human activity has been recognised through the ages from as far back as the time of the ancient Egyptian writings on the Papyrus. No one can deny that cycles occur in human behaviour, just as there are cycles in natural growth. The seasons, spring, summer, autumn and winter, appear as regularly as the rising and setting of the sun. And what is true with Nature is true with Man. Certain animal instincts lying deep down in Man's being are stirred at given seasons according to the natural rhythm of his growth. Despite all our civilisation to-day, we are still occasionally moved by our animal instincts.'

Craig said:

'Are you kidding?'

The Professor said, earnestly:

'People may pretend to be very nice and kind, but underneath it all they are just animals.'

He paused. The idea seemed to have struck some disagreeable chord in his memory. For a moment Craig thought hopefully he was going to drop the whole business and fade. The Professor, however, pulled himself together and went on:

'I am making a chart showing the number of murders which have been committed at the full moon during the last thirty years. Certain kinds of people, you know, lose their sense of proportion under the influence of the moon.'

'Certain kinds of people, you know, lose their sense of proportion at any time,' Craig murmured.

'Quite, quite. This — er — moon madness is called insanity nowadays. But that is only one of those labels civilisation fixes on to anything it fails to understand. I know it to be Man's return to the primitive, a perfectly natural state of being. People can say what they like, but

Man's behaviour is fundamentally governed by primitive emotions. My wife agrees with me on that point.'

Craig said:

'I didn't know you were married.'

'Oh, yes.'

Again he paused as if some unpleasant memory had returned to him. Again it seemed he might give up the object of his visit and drift off. Again Craig was disappointed.

'I am about to tell you the most interesting part of the idea,' the Professor said with impressive glibness. 'I have divided men and women into twelve different types. The divisions are partly based on the times of birth and the twelve signs of the Zodiac, but I also include the influence of the endocrine glands. Believe me, I can always fit anyone into one of my twelve types. Most interesting. Every person I meet is just a type to me.'

'That must make life very cosy for you.'

'You, for instance, are a Leo. You were born in August.'

Craig looked at him with interest.

'Pretty good.'

The Professor smiled deprecatingly.

'It is nothing.' He continued warmly: 'Now this is the crux of the matter. I have arrived at the conclusion that fanatical persons who, when under the certain endocrine influences to which I have alluded, are potential murderers, have Scorpio for their birth sign.'

'Who?'

'Scorpio,' the Professor replied patiently. 'Scorpio is the ruling sign which has prompted crimes of passion, murder and hate. It would be no exaggeration to say that in most cases where crimes have been committed in paroxysms of inflamed passion and insane jealousy, Scorpio will be dominating the horoscope of the criminals concerned.'

Craig yawned ostentatiously and asked him:

'What exactly would you be driving at?'

'It is this Scorpio type to which I have referred who would be most likely to obey their baser and grosser instincts when under the influence of a full moon.' The Professor's voice rose dramatically. 'If, in addition, these persons possess certain physical characteristics, their actions under these circumstances are almost invariably simple to prognosticate.' He paused and his tone became more casual: 'If, as I understand by the reports that have been appearing in one of the more popular newspapers, you are interested in solving the Maida Vale murder, I can reveal to you the identity of the person responsible forthwith.'

'This should be good,' Craig told him. 'Spill it.'

'The man you are looking for has dark hair, brown eyes set in a fixed stare, a narrow forehead and was born on November the nineteenth.'

The Professor took off his spectacles and blinked at Craig triumphantly.

'You amaze me,' Craig said. 'Thanks a lot.'

'Not at all,' the other assured him.

'My secretary has your address if I should want to consult you?'

'I gave it her the last time I was here. I will give it her again on my way out.'

'Do that little thing.'

At the door the Professor turned and

replaced his spectacles.

'Needless to say,' he murmured over his bowler hat, 'my expert assistance is always at your disposal.' And he went out.

Craig shook his head and lit a cigarette. He hadn't the heart to tell the Professor that he'd always been under the impression his birthday was in March.

9

After the door closed behind the Professor, Craig dragged at his cigarette for a moment, then he dialled a number. He was put through to Gabriel Warwick's secretary.

The murder of Lucy Evans had pushed Gabriel Warwick's invitation out of his mind. Now he remembered it and the job that might be on the end of it.

Mr. Warwick's engagement diary was very, very full, his secretary told him and she was afraid she couldn't squeeze him in for a couple of days. Afternoon. Craig said, all right, it would be very nice of her to squeeze him in then, and hung up. He idly watched the smoke curl up from his cigarette, then crossed to the door, listened for a moment and opened it.

'The menace has gone,' Simone said to him. 'Do you want to know what he told me?'

'If you don't think I'm too young to know.'

'He says I am a Sagittarius.'

His eyes travelled over her.

'I always warned you the way you curved in the right places gave men the wrong impressions.' He moved towards the other door. 'I'm on my way.'

Even when she pulled a face at him she still looked very luscious. She said:

'You should be interested in my horoscope.'

He said to her:

'Not just now. Time and place for everything.'

'And what are you interested in just now?'

'The South London Property Development Company.'

The offices were on the second floor of a big corner block. Three girls were working in the main office. Written on a frosted-glass door at the back was: 'Mr. Anthony Webber, General Manager.'

The girl operating the switchboard had a copy of the *Globe* propped up before her. She was staring hard at the photograph of Lucy Evans. Craig stood there for a moment or two before she condescended to look up. Then she gave him a saccharine smile.

'Yes?'

Craig nodded towards the inner office.

'Would he be at home?'

'Have you an appointment?'

She patted her hair and started to work her charm overtime.

Craig grinned at her gently. With a quick glance round he leaned forward, heavily conspiratorial. He said:

'Not exactly. The name's Craig. I'm a private detective.'

She should have lapped it up. Instead, she relaxed doing her charm stuff and her expression sharpened. She stared at him hard before asking:

'Have you come about Lucy?'

He eyed her blandly.

'I want to ask your Mr. Webber a thing or two about someone who used to work for him.'

'Come off it,' she said. 'You mean Lucy Evans.'

Craig shrugged with a little smile.

'I can see you're too bright for me.'

She indicated a chair.

'You can take the weight off your feet if you like. I'll go and see if he's disengaged.'

She let him have her long, sweet smile again. She was smart, trim and had a little turned-up nose. Craig watched the seams on the backs of her sheer stockings as she disappeared into Webber's office.

She was back a moment later. Mr. Webber would give him five minutes of his time. Just like that.

Craig grinned at her and went in, feeling her eyes on the back of his neck. He found himself in a large, well-furnished room. It was more of a room than an office. A couple of choice oils adorned the walls, and there were plenty of flowers around.

Webber didn't bother to get up from his swivel-chair behind the wide desk. With a pale, well-shaped hand he indicated Craig to grab himself a seat.

'Now, Mr. Craig, what can I do for you? I'm afraid I can only give you a few minutes. I have a conference.'

Craig didn't wait for him to ask him to take a cigarette from the large silver box before him. He lit it slowly and a little frown marred the other's brow. Craig drew at his cigarette appreciatively. It was an expensive brand and he thought Anthony Webber showed excellent taste.

Webber spoke again, his tone definitely edgy.

'I suppose you've come to ask me if I can tell you anything about this unfortunate girl? Frankly, I know very little about her. She worked here as my secretary until just over a week ago. Then she resigned. She gave me to understand she had other prospects in view. I was sorry to lose her. She was an efficient worker. I'm afraid that is all I can tell you.'

Craig eyed the tip of his cigarette. He said slowly:

'I was wondering if it could be you knew the character she was going around with.'

The other's frown had disappeared. He placed the tips of his fingers together and smiled urbanely.

'I have to admit I was not aware she had formed any attachment of the kind to which you refer, but, you see, I do not in the nature of things have very much contact with the private lives of our employees. I'm sorry to disappoint you.'

Craig didn't say anything. There was a little silence and Webber began to tap his finger-tips together. He took no pains to disguise the fact that he was waiting for Craig to go.

Craig didn't move.

The other stirred uneasily. He cleared his throat and said:

'Tell me, Mr. Craig, is it your idea that this poor girl may have been murdered by this — ah — friend? That is to say, if there is one.'

Craig regarded him thoughtfully.

'He'd make a sort of a useful witness.'

Anthony Webber nodded slowly.

'I see. I wish I could help you more, but I'm afraid I can't. If anything should occur to me, I will of course contact you immediately.'

This time he stood up and held out his hand. His grip was firm. Craig allowed himself to be impelled to the door. As the other opened it he said, casually:

'You would say Lucy Evans appeared

perfectly normal on the day she left you? Or wouldn't you say?'

Webber paused a moment without turning the doorhandle before replying.

'If you mean, did she appear in any way — ah — distressed, I would certainly say no.' Again that tiny frown drew his brows together. 'Since you mention it, my recollection seems to be that she appeared quite elated. Almost, you might say, as if she were excited about something.'

'Almost, you might say, like a girl who was going to be married?'

The slight frown was no longer there.

'It hadn't occurred to me, but yes — ' he hesitated, 'yes, that's what she might have looked like.'

'She have any relatives in London? She ever refer to anyone?'

Webber was opening the door.

'Really, I don't know. She might have had, but I can't remember her mentioning anyone to me. Now, Mr. Craig,' he said briskly, 'I don't think there is anything more I can do for you. As I said, if I should recall any little incident, you can rely on me to let you know.'

The door closed.

The girl turned from the switchboard as Craig slowly approached. Her mouth was freshly lipsticked. She looked up at him inquiringly.

'How did you make out?'

'Interesting talker, your Mr. Webber.'

'He would be if he said anything.'

'You've noticed that, too?'

She shrugged.

'After all, that's what he's paid for.'

He let his hand drop carelessly on her shoulder. She didn't move away.

'I wonder — ?'

'You wonder what?' Her voice was full of innuendo. 'Maybe I could help you?'

'I think you could.' He tapped the ash off his cigarette. 'You wouldn't happen to have a specimen of Lucy Evans' handwriting?'

She shot him a look of surprise, then she stood up.

'Pardon me,' she said, brushing past him closely. In a moment she was back with a ledger.

Craig flipped through the pages. Descriptions of various properties were written on the left-hand side and there were figures in the right-hand column. The writing was small and regular. Obviously the same as that of the unfinished letter he'd found in the Maida Vale bed-sitting-room. It clinched the idea that it had been written by Lucy Evans. It meant, without a doubt, that the nebulous lover really did exist.

He snapped the ledger shut and handed it back to the girl. As she took it, her fingers contrived to close over his and she made no attempt to draw them away.

'When you've finished with my hand,' he said bleakly.

'I'm so sorry,' she breathed, her eyes very wide and warm.

He stared back at her unwinkingly. He said:

'Who was her boy-friend?'

'Do you mean the one from the insurance company?' she said at once. Craig didn't bat an eyelash, and she went on: 'I think he was the real one in the running, though I wouldn't say for certain. Lucy didn't talk a lot about men. This one came in one day to see him,' she

65

nodded over her shoulder towards the door. 'That was how Lucy met him. He was a pretty fast worker, come to think of it. He rang up half an hour after he'd gone. He wanted to speak to her. I think he made a date with her for that night and she went out with him. That was the beginning of it, I know, and my idea was she was keen about him. But, as I say, I can't really tell.'

'What did he look like?'

'Youngish, darkish, I think. I wouldn't like to say. I didn't notice properly. He wasn't my type.'

She stared at him blatantly. She was a little closer and Craig thought the perfume she wore was very nice. He asked, with elaborate casualness:

'His name?'

She thought about it for a moment and finally shook her head.

'I don't ever remember hearing his name.'

'How about that time Lucy first met him?' he suggested.

She shook her head again.

'The boss was expecting him and Lucy

66

took him straight in. Why don't you ask Mr. Webber?'

Craig had already thought of that, though he didn't think it necessary. The idea that the girl had been talking about Jeffrey Brook loomed up more and more convincingly in his mind. He tried to dismiss it as being too far-fetched, but all the same, a lot of little circumstances were fitting together. There was something off-key about Helen March. Her anxiety over Brook drifting off and leaving her last night. The very night, and around the time, when Lucy Evans had been bumped off. And there had been the missing button, too. It wasn't conclusive, but it was there, naggingly fitting in with the other details. And now here was this girl telling him that Lucy's number one boy-friend worked for an insurance firm.

'Could all these things be coincidental?' Craig asked himself. He said to the girl:

'Would you know who he worked for?'

'Mr. Webber could tell you that, too.'

He eyed her through a cloud of tobacco-smoke. He said:

'Don't think I'll be bothering him, somehow. His memory's inclined to be patchy. Would it be Pyramid Assurance?'

She shrugged her slim shoulders. Then she said:

'Pyramid Assurance. Yes, that was it. It comes back to me. If anything else comes back to me,' she offered, 'where do I find you?'

He gave her his number. She was a nice kid. 'I'll probably be looking in on you again,' he told her.

'I can hardly wait.'

'I know,' he said.

He went down in the lift with plenty to think about. As the gates opened he almost barged into a man who was standing waiting. The other muttered an apology and Craig gave him a swift glance. He had Scotland Yard written all over him in neons a foot high.

Craig went on out into the street.

10

Helen could hear Jeff moving around in the little bathroom.

She didn't worry about Jeff now. It was useless to make herself ill with vague fears that might turn out to be imaginary. She must settle down to her new life and try to keep an open mind.

She hadn't said anything to him about the girl who'd been found strangled in Maida Vale. Perhaps after all it wasn't the same girl she'd seen with him that night. She couldn't be sure of it, so she buried the idea away. She determined to forget all about the whole thing.

She couldn't believe she had been married only a couple of days. Already marriage was giving her ordinary practical problems to keep her busy enough. She wanted to make Jeff's small flat more comfortable for him than it had been when he occupied it alone. She wanted to impress her own personality upon it and make it a home for them. Their first home together. His business friends would, she planned, visit them often and approve of her good taste. One of the duties of the modern wife was to form a background to her husband's career. She hoped she would be able to feel, when Jeff became successful, that she had helped him on the way.

She went into the bathroom.

'Breakfast, darling.'

Jeff's face was half hidden under a foam of shaving-soap. The morning ritual of shaving was a serious business with him. Sometimes he shaved at night as well. He had an unusually strong, dark beard, which grew as fast as he could razor it off.

He turned to her.

'Be there in a few minutes.'

He lathered soap over his face and she was fascinated. She put an arm round him and he kissed her, leaving blobs of white lather clinging to her nose and cheek.

'Jeff, how are we going to keep being like this always? Can't we make a pact or something to swear we'll never stop being in love? I mean, so that if things ever do go wrong we could always remember how we feel to-day and things would go right again.'

He laughed at her gently. He said:

'Things are not going to go wrong. I married you because I wanted you and I usually know what I want.'

'You're always so certain, so sure of yourself. Don't you ever get a bit afraid sometimes?'

He said, darkly:

'I'm afraid now. I'm afraid my shaving water will get cold.'

Helen smiled at him happily and went back into the living-room. Presently he appeared in a dressing-gown. They faced each other across the blue-and-white check cloth and she poured coffee.

'How did you get on last night?' she asked conversationally. 'Was it a success-ful dinner?'

He hesitated a moment before he said:

'Very successful. Very successful indeed.' Then he added: 'By the way, anyone 'phone me after I'd gone last night?' He sounded just a little too casual.

'No. Why? Who would it be?' He asked the same question yesterday. Had anyone 'phoned while he'd been away from the flat.

'Nobody.' He brushed it aside. 'Just a small matter. Listen, darling, I have a surprise for you. I got some good news last night. It was at the dinner. We're going to be pretty well-off pretty soon.'

'That's going to be nice,' she smiled at him. She wasn't taking him too seriously.

'I'm not kidding.'

She realised he was being very serious about it. Obediently she stopped smiling and asked him:

'Is it the job Mr. Warwick spoke about?'

He nodded:

'We're going to move out of here, darling. It's too small. We shall have enough money to live as I've always wanted to live.'

She stared at him.

'Move out of here? But, Jeff — '

'I've had my eye on a place down in the country. Not far from town. I want to show it you. We'll go down to-day in the car. I've taken the morning off from the office.'

So that was why he hadn't worried about hurrying off to the office. Helen was amazed at this sudden news, though she had always known that Jeff was heading for a big job, and intended moving somewhere into the country the moment he could afford it. She brushed away a shadow that grew at the back of her mind. She looked out of the window. It was a bright morning and the prospect of a drive out into the fresh air certainly appeared good. If she thought it a little strange Jeff should spring the surprise so suddenly, any lingering misgivings were soon dispersed by the sunshine.

'Oh, Jeff, you're wonderful,' she said.

A little while later they were speeding along the St. John's Wood Road, across Maida Vale, past Paddington Station and so to the Bayswater Road. Soon they were on the wide arterial road at Brentford. The Great West Road.

Jeff trod on the accelerator and coaxed the little car up to fifty miles an hour. The wind rushed past and Helen's hair streamed out and she liked it. The sun and the wind and the ever-opening road ahead gave her a strange exhilaration. She smiled a special smile to herself.

In half an hour they were well out of London and going through Slough. Then a flat stretch of main road opened up before them. Windsor Castle could be seen across the fields to the south.

'Where is the house?'

'Not far now,' he told her.

His gaze was fixed steadily on the road in front.

They came to a junction and he seemed uncertain whether they should take the side road or not. He made up his mind. Apparently it wasn't the way he was looking for. He accelerated again. A few minutes later they came to another side-road, to the right, leading up to a wooded hill. They turned here and soon they were speeding up the hill. A canopy of trees spread right over the road, making green tunnels in places.

Jeff was sure of his way now. Helen glanced at him a little puzzled at the intentness of his face. He didn't seem to notice she was looking at him. At last he turned the car down a narrow lane at the end of which there was a gate. Lying back among the trees was an old Victorian-looking house. There were tall ground-floor windows and pillars at the front-door porch. It was a rambling place, built of dull red brick, very much discoloured.

Jeff got out and opened the gate, then drove the car through. The house came more fully into view as they went up the drive and it was soon evident it was empty. The car pulled up outside the front door.

Helen stared at it for a moment. Then: 'It's a bit gloomy.'

He didn't answer. He was staring at the top windows and seemed to be deep in thought, or perhaps listening. It was very quiet. Helen looked back down the drive and then at the trees that overshadowed it. She turned her gaze to the house again. With its gables and out-houses it was as if there was something about it knocking at her memory. It was strange the way it knocked at her. She had the curious impression she had seen it before. Yet she knew this was impossible. She could never have seen it before.

'Jeff,' she whispered.

He shot a look at her and she snuggled up to him.

'What's the matter?'

'It's silly of me,' she smiled. 'Don't take any notice.'

A bird flew off towards a belt of trees and the sudden cry it gave disturbed the stillness. From somewhere a long way off came the chop-chop as of someone cutting wood. Occasionally the wind made a faint rushing noise among the leaves above them.

Jeff stirred and said:

'Quiet, isn't it? Matter of fact, we're about three miles from the main road. The village is about two miles away. There are one or two big houses nearer than that.'

She thought he seemed to be watching her as if to see what she was thinking. Then he got out of the car and she followed him. He produced a key and marched up to the front door.

'I hope you like it inside. You must allow for the place being a bit neglected.'

The door swung back.

They found themselves in a wide hall with a staircase at the end. The carpet was down, but the furniture was covered with big, white dust-sheets, giving the place a desolate air.

'I want you to see all the rooms.'

He was tremendously keen to show her the new home he had chosen. He wanted her to like it. She smiled at him and took his arm. She was determined to make herself like it to please him. He said, shyly:

'I thought this would make up for our not going away on a honeymoon.'

She pressed his arm and looked up at him tremulously. He bent and kissed her.

They went upstairs and made their way from room to room. Their footsteps echoed through the silent house. There were four rooms on the first floor and the same number on the second. One of the attic rooms on the top floor appeared to be locked. Going downstairs again, they explored the kitchen and servants' quarters at the back.

Jeff said:

'We could run this with a man and his wife living in.'

He was planning ahead. He was talking his thoughts aloud. She tried desperately to attune herself to his mood. He looked at her.

'How would you like to live here?'

She knew she must accept the change of home as a part of her destiny and she was prepared to like it.

'I think I will love it.' He grinned at her boyishly. She said: 'But don't you think it a little early yet to be moving into the country. Don't you have to be on the board of directors, or something, before you can do that?'

'It's usual,' he laughed.

They went out to look at the garden at the back. The trees grew even more thickly than in front. A lawn lay between the trees and the house. It was heavily overgrown with weeds.

'Those woods over there,' he was saying, 'slope down to the river. We're right on top of the hill here, you know. If you go down the hill a mile or so you come to the river. They have sailing there in the summer.'

She nodded, but her mind was on other things.

'Jeff, are you sure we can afford all this?'

He eyed her narrowly.

'I can afford it now.'

For the first time since he had sprung the surprise on her that morning, Helen felt in her heart the sudden change in Jeff's circumstances was not natural.

It was true Pyramid Assurance had for some time been promising him a better job, but it was obvious a large sum of money would be needed to buy this house. More than he could earn in salary, unless it had been increased fantastically.

She felt a return of that fear she thought she was beginning to banish for ever. It was with her again, sending her into a sickening panic the same as when she had seen the photograph of the blonde girl in the newspaper. She couldn't help feeling Jeff was hiding something from her. She couldn't help feeling his replies were evasive and concealed some secret purpose.

She forced herself to listen to him as he

began speaking again.

'This is all so worth-while. Somewhere to live where no one can disturb you. It's worth having and once you've got it, no one can take it away. It's yours.'

He turned to her almost urgently. 'D'you see what I mean, darling? We need a place like this. We couldn't look forward to grubbing along in my little flat. Supposing I buy this place, how do you feel about living out here? It's quiet, I know. But you can get to town easily and quickly.'

She tried to control her voice and make it sound casual. She said, with a shaky laugh:

'What are you going to use for money?'

'I've already told you.' His tone was taut, almost harsh. There was a sense of strain about the line of his jaw. 'I've got a big job now. We shall have enough to keep us going. And — and apart from that, I had a legacy left me. An uncle. I've been keeping it for this.' He laughed a little and his jaw-line softened. 'Something I was hiding from you. A secret I didn't want you to know about until now.'

She looked at him, a wave of relief flooding her.

He made it sound reasonable enough. Why shouldn't he have had some money left him? She began to realise that once again she had been wrong and stupid to doubt him.

They were rounding a corner of the house and then, as they came in sight of their car, Helen suddenly felt her arm gripped as Jeff pulled her back into the shadow of a tree. He was staring at the house and the question on Helen's lips died as she followed his fixed gaze.

A woman stood at the front door. She wore a long, grey cloak. She was tall and appeared old and thin.

'Who is she?'

Her whisper broke off as his grip on her arm tightened warningly.

The woman turned and began to move away. She moved away down the drive like a wraith, a grey shape that was soon lost in the tunnel of the trees. She might have been nothing more than a figure of illusion.

'Who is she?' Helen asked again.

Jeff shrugged, his eyes remaining riveted on the spot where the woman had vanished. He said, still without moving his gaze:

'Haven't the vaguest idea.'

She turned to him and tried to read what lay beyond his sombre eyes, but she couldn't, not while he refused to help her like this.

Jeff said:

'Let's get back to town.'

11

Detective-Inspector Marraby sat at his desk chewing on a cold pipe. He looked up as Craig came in and waved him into a chair. It was the first chance he'd given Craig to drop in on him since their last meeting at Vale Crescent.

'I'll say this for you, Craig, you don't come any funny business like trying to out-smart Scotland Yard. That's the sort of thing makes trouble. We can't be everywhere at once, naturally, but if anybody picks up some information, their job is to bring it to us and not try and score off us by selling it to the newspapers. I don't mind telling you, if it had been one of those crime reporters he would have tried to be clever and used the story for himself. You're different, of course. You're a detective. Even if you do play a lone hand.'

Craig grinned at him.

This was the way he wanted it to go.

This was the way he always played it with the Scotland Yard crowd. He didn't run around like those clever-clever sleuths that figure in books, always showing up the police for a bunch of nit-wits. He knew none came smarter than the boys of the Criminal Investigation Department and so long as he wanted to run his business for profit, it paid him to keep in their good books.

Marraby went on exercising his jaw muscles.

'I'll tell you something, Craig. We're planning to clean up crime. Definitely. But we can't do it without help. Help from the public. The apathy of the public is one of our greatest stumbling-blocks. We don't get any help anywhere. The only time they take any notice of us is when some smart newspaperman tries to make fools of us. Then the public laugh. That doesn't do any good, Craig. That's why I'm glad you still go on playing ball with us.' He nodded with slow approval. Craig waited for him to go on talking. Marraby said: 'Now, then, just what is this snippet of information you think might help us?'

Craig lit a cigarette.

'I've always worked in with you, as you know,' he said. 'All the same, it's nice to hear you say you appreciate it. Personally, I can't understand why other people don't act the same. But that's not my worry. I've got worries of my own.'

'What's this information?' Marraby said, a touch of impatience in his tone. 'What's on your mind?'

Craig hesitated a moment. This was it. The old so-and-so opposite him wasn't going to be softened up by any man to-man stuff. He said:

'I've had a theory about this Maida Vale business from the moment you invited me in on it.'

Marraby gave a cough, but let it go. It wasn't much encouragement, but Craig continued.

'My theory was that this was another of those crimes where the girl's been turned down by her boyfriend. She's threatened to make things sticky for him if he refuses to marry her, or maybe hand over some cash. But maybe he's married already, or has a job to consider, or is mean over money. Anyway, the only way out for him is to keep the girl quiet. Permanently.'

The other was watching him intently. He took his pipe out of his mouth and put it on the desk. He said:

'Go on.'

'I got this slant on the set-up on account of the note I found. You remember? It said how she was always thinking of him. How he didn't 'phone. How he'd better keep his promise. Or else. She threatened she'd put in a squeak about him.'

Marraby shifted restlessly.

'Here's what I'm getting at,' Craig said quickly. 'The man who was heard visiting Lucy Evans that night might have been any man. But the evidence of the letter seems to indicate he was her boy-friend number one. Now, what I've been asking myself is this: Did Lucy Evans in fact write that letter? How do we know she wrote it? We are assuming she did, but supposing it was written by someone else? What difference would that make in your life? Wait a minute,' he proceeded smoothly as the other hunched forward to speak. 'Wait a minute. I am able to tell you that our assumption is in fact right on the button. I have established, without a shadow of doubt, that Lucy Evans did write that letter. I have seen her handwriting at the office where she worked.'

Marraby pushed back his chair angrily.

'For Pete's sake, Craig,' he grunted, his perpetually aggrieved expression darkened by a scowl, 'that ruddy landlady identified it as Lucy Evans' handwriting at the time.'

Craig registered the appropriate amount of chagrin, and told himself it hadn't come off.

Admittedly it was a long shot that Marraby wouldn't have thought of showing the letter to the landlady for identification purposes. But he might possibly have slipped up on it. Smarter detectives had overlooked such obvious routine checking up before now.

If Marraby had missed it, Craig's information clinching that Lucy Evans had in fact written the letter would certainly have chalked up one more debt of gratitude to Craig's credit. But he had been unlucky this time.

He had realised the last couple of days the weakness of his position so far as the Maida Vale case went was that he was not working for a client actually involved in the mystery. He had barged into it simply as a side-issue of his *Globe* assignment to investigate the fire outbreaks. He was playing a hunch, however, that there was more to Lucy Evans' murder than appeared on the surface. What it was, exactly, he couldn't tie a label to, but if he worried it enough, he'd write out the tag sooner or later.

It was therefore essential for his purpose he should keep in with Marraby. Without his co-operation he might miss vital tip-offs which, added to the information he dug up himself, could easily give him all he wanted to know. Well, he hadn't pulled anything out of the bag this time. But maybe he'd get another break to ingratiate himself with Marraby.

Best thing he could do now was to get out before the Inspector threw him out. He gave the other a rueful grin.

'Just to save you wasting my time again,' Marraby was rasping, 'I've checked up at the place where the girl worked, too.'

Craig didn't say anything. Just hoped the other would go on talking a bit more. The Inspector obliged. He went on:

'Not that they were able to tell us anything there, anyway.'

Craig regarded him unblinkingly. He smiled to himself. He'd picked up that much from Marraby, at any rate. Anthony Webber hadn't been a lot of help to him, either. He wondered how much Webber had talked to the police without saying anything.

On his way from Marraby's office, he found himself pondering idly on the girl with the tip-tilted nose who operated the switchboard at the South London Property Development Company.

12

Some time later Craig swung his feet on to his desk and tilted back his chair. Simone asked him:

'How did it work?'

He shook his head.

'I should have thought up something better,' he told her, watching the smoke of his cigarette curl ceilingwards. He mentioned the crumb of information Marraby had let fall and she said it was something anyway, and he said:

'What ideas have you about Jeffrey Brook? Think there's something funny going on there?'

She looked at him. He had not said anything to Simone about the notion that had been taking shape in his mind about Brook.

'Does there have to be anything funny about him?'

'There doesn't *have* to be anything funny about Jeffrey Brook, except that at the same time he's been running around with Helen March he's also been friendly with a little blonde named Lucy Evans. And on the night the little blonde is murdered in Maida Vale, and around the same time, our Mr. Brook, in the middle of drinks he's having with the girl he's going to marry and one or two others, suddenly leaves to meet a man about a business deal.'

'You mean he was really meeting the girl who was murdered? It sounds fantastic. How do you know he even knew her?'

'Lucy Evans was done in by the man she thought she was going to marry. He was running out on her, so she threatened to squeak about something, and he gave her the works. That's the hunch I've had all along. So to-day I make inquiries at the office where Lucy Evans worked. I find out her number one boyfriend is employed by Pyramid Assurance.'

She gave a little gasp.

'I know,' he said. 'Comes as quite a surprise, doesn't it?'

'All the same, it doesn't prove he is Jeffrey Brook.'

'All right,' he nodded, 'let's call it all circumstantial stuff. Even the coat-button that was found near the body. It had got torn off in the struggle.' He paused, then added: 'When Jeffrey Brook was leaving with Helen March that night after I'd returned, I noticed he had a button missing from his coat. But let's just say that's circumstantial, too.'

'It is unbelievable. I wonder — ?' She broke off, then she said: 'Helen did not seem very happy that evening. I do not know her very well, of course. Getting married may take her that way. Or was it that she suspected Jeffrey Brook was playing around with someone else?' She shook her head slowly, as if she found the idea impossible. 'Would it be a good thing,' she said, 'if I had a chat with Helen, just casually? I might find out something.'

'She seemed satisfied enough with the excuse he gave her about his business appointment. You bet he'll have made all the explanation necessary. No. You'd only risk letting him know that I know.'

'What are you going to do?'

He was scowling slightly to himself.

'What I would like to know is, what is it that girl knew about him which she was going to use if he walked out on her?'

'Perhaps it is all a coincidence,' she said hopefully.

'Maybe it could be that, too,' he shrugged. But he didn't sound as if he really believed it.

That afternoon Craig walked into the mahogany-panelled vestibule of the Pyramid Assurance building. A very old commissionaire tottered towards him and Craig told him who he was. He thought the whole atmosphere of the place was mellow, ripe with the tradition of big business.

'This way, sir.'

Craig followed the commissionaire to the lift.

Gabriel Warwick's office smelled of old leather. The arm-chairs were leather, the walls were lined with books bound in leather, the heavy desk was inlaid with leather. Gabriel Warwick rose and held out his hand. Here in his office he was seen against a background that made him appear most impressive. His geniality, which had been so apparent at the Café Rouge, seemed subdued somewhat by a business-like briskness as he greeted Craig.

'Good afternoon, Mr. Craig. I am very glad you looked in.'

Craig took a cigarette from the box which was pushed across to him and lit it. Gabriel Warwick paced over to the windows and stood for a moment looking down at the street before he turned and said:

'We have employed private investigators now and again, of course, but I haven't been altogether satisfied about a number of fire claims that Pyramid Assurance has had to meet during the past several months.' He paused and went on: 'I am not suggesting that the detective agencies we have employed have given anything but their best services. It's simply that I feel a fresh approach might yield better results.'

Craig, speaking for practically the first time, said:

'I think our little chat is slightly at cross-purposes.'

Gabriel Warwick glanced at him, his gaze suddenly narrow.

'You see,' Craig told him, 'I haven't come about the job you offered me the other evening.'

'Then what have you come about?'

Craig ignored the query, continuing:

'Since then the *Globe* has kept my nose to the grindstone. Not only fire, but a nice slice of homicide. All of which would leave me no time at all to handle anything for your firm. This little visit is about something else again.'

'I'm sorry you can't see your way to work for us, Mr. Craig,' the other said, smoothly. 'However, some other time, possibly.'

'Why not?' Craig smiled at him.

'Meanwhile, perhaps you'd explain the real object of your visit?'

Craig tapped the ash off his cigarette. He eyed Gabriel Warwick carefully for a moment. Then he said, simply:

'Jeffrey Brook.'

The other frowned at him with surprise.

'One or two questions I'd like to ask

you about him. Naturally I shall treat anything you say in strictest confidence,' he added glibly.

'I really don't see — ' Gabriel Warwick began. Then he broke off and stared at Craig intently, still with the puzzled frown. 'What interest have you in Mr. Brook?'

'I mentioned a little matter of murder,' Craig told him and the other started. Craig went on coolly: 'I may be wrong. I hope I am. But I formed the impression that Jeffrey Brook could spill some pretty useful information about it.'

'Brook implicated in a murder? But that's impossible.' Gabriel Warwick shifted uneasily in his chair, his frown deepening. 'What makes you think that?'

'You've known him a long time?'

The other hesitated. His expression indicated plainly the idea a member of his firm could be involved in anything so unsavoury as a murder was extremely distasteful to him. He said:

'Let me see. About a year.'

'A year. Not so long. I somehow had the impression he'd been with you much longer.'

'Brook's an experienced man,' the other said, as if in explanation. 'One of my best men. Most of his experience was gained with another company. The City Star Insurance Company. They were about to promote him to London supervisor of the fire department.'

'Why did he leave?'

'The City Star went bankrupt a year back.' Gabriel Warwick shook his head. 'Most regrettable affair. They over-insured. An unusual number of large claims came in and they were unable to realise their securities in time to avoid a panic.'

Craig didn't bat an eyelash. This is something else, he thought, wondering what he'd stumble on next. He said:

'Were these large claims by any chance fire claims?'

'I don't know. I believe some of them were.'

Craig nodded and dragged at his cigarette.

'So Jeffrey Brook was with City Star and City Star crashed and you took him on. Is that right?'

The other nodded.

'Why did you take him on?'

Gabriel Warwick regarded him for a moment, then pressed a button on his desk. A girl came in.

'Let me have the personal staff file regarding Mr. Jeffrey Brook.'

'Yes, Mr. Warwick.'

In a moment she returned with the file, which Gabriel Warwick took and flipped through quickly. The letter which he handed Craig was a short note, typewritten beneath City Star Insurance Company heading.

'*Dear Mr. Warwick,*

Further to our telephone conversation, I am sending you a member of our staff who has always given most excellent service. I cannot speak too highly of Mr. Jeffrey Brook.

Mr. Brook's qualifications speak for themselves, while his integrity, efficiency and knowledge of the insurance business have been of estimable value to us in the past and will, I am sure, prove of value to you in the future.

Yours very truly,

Stanley Broadhurst.'

Craig noticed the date. It was a year before.

'Stanley Broadhurst was managing-director of City Star,' Gabriel Warwick was saying. 'He practically owned the firm. It wasn't a very big concern. He lost his entire fortune when it wound up. It was a ghastly blow.' He paused for a moment reminiscently. 'Poor chap committed suicide. A very sad business.'

There was a little silence.

'Jeffrey Brook certainly seems the enthusiastic type,' Craig said.

'Meaning what?'

'I was thinking of his leaving the party that night because of a business appointment he'd fixed up. Must have been quite a deal to take him away on an evening like that. Incidentally, did he pull it off?'

The other answered him evasively.

'I can't quite recall the particular business that was occupying his attention at that time. But, as you say, Brook is on top of his job all the time.' He permitted himself a faint smile. 'Even, as you suggest, on the night before his wedding.'

Craig didn't pursue the subject and a

few minutes later he was on his way out of the office. A young man was going into another office as Craig approached the lift. His good-looking face was carefully shaved, his tie expertly knotted.

'Hello,' said Jeffrey Brook, recognising Craig after a momentary flash of surprise.

'I must call you some time,' Craig said smoothly. 'I must get you to explain about this life insurance.'

'Of course,' Jeffrey Brook said easily. 'Though, as a matter of fact I'm working on the fire section. But I'd put you on to the right chap, with pleasure.'

'Fine. We must get together.'

The other smiled good-bye and Craig stood and watched the office door close behind him.

Presently, back in his own office, Craig was saying into the telephone:

'Bill Holt?'

'What is it, Nat?'

'Listen, Bill. I want the case history of a character named Jeffrey Brook who used to be employed by the City Star Insurance Company before it went down the drain about a year ago.'

'Okay.'

'One thing more. There was a fire in Shoreditch a few nights back. Paper-bag firm.'

'The East London Paper Carton Company.'

'Dig up for me the name of the insurance policy holder. While you're on that, do the same for me on the Park View Hotel, Richmond.'

'Anything else you want?'

'That'll do for now.'

'Okay, Nat. I'll be ringing you back.'

Craig hung up.

It was just before nine o'clock that evening when it happened. The tip-off from the *Globe* about a building on fire near the Elephant and Castle. A large silk-goods warehouse going up in smoke. Yes, the *Globe* told Craig, the place was blazing beautifully.

13

Craig's taxi headed towards the red glow in the sky. Dodging round the side-streets, they missed the fire engines, the ambulances and the crowds hurrying to the fire.

It was a terrifying sight. A large warehouse, its frontage on the main street, but with most of its area lying back beyond the other buildings, was a mass of red and yellow fire. Sparks shot up against the dark sky as more and more of the woodwork was gripped in the licking flames. A deep roar as the consuming holocaust spread over its prey was punctuated by the crackling of wood and the sudden rumbling of falling masonry.

More fire engines arrived, their bells clanging, and pushed through the milling crowd. Police cars edged through the sea of human faces showing up red and pink in the ever-changing light. Fainting women, crushed by the surge of spectators, were lifted over heads to reach the ambulances. The whole scene was vivid with colours, red and yellow, deep blue and black.

The concerted efforts of the fire brigades were beginning to have some effect on the blaze. It was too late to save the warehouse itself. Flames had got too firm a grip, had spread to every corner. But the fire was being successfully isolated and headed off from neighbouring buildings.

A deep rumbling, a sudden burst of flame skyward and a colossal shower of sparks told the roof was collapsing. Smoke belched out over the crowd. Half the roof was gone already. Now the rest was slipping rapidly. A final tower of flame, a noise like a long roll of thunder, and what was left of the warehouse roof vanished.

'Good job nobody's in there,' an ambulance man muttered in Craig's ear.

'How did it start?'

'Dunno. But they got the caretaker over there by that police-car.'

Craig pushed his way over. He was in time to hear the caretaker, a grizzled, distraught-looking little man, reaching the end of his account of what had happened.

'I was drinking me cup of tea and having me first lot of sannidges when I hears this noise like wood crackling. Soon as I opens the door to go along the main corridor I could smell what it was. What beat me was how it spread so quick. By the time I'd 'phoned the fire station, the whole ruddy place was up in flames.'

Craig spotted a fire brigade officer he knew and moved over to him.

'Kind of a boom in trade for you,' he said.

The other nodded, mopping the perspiration off his face with a large handkerchief.

'How d'you imagine this little flare-up started?'

'That's what puzzled us a bit at first. The fire spread unusually fast. We didn't have much chance to see its beginnings.'

'Any idea?'

'Maybe. One of my men found the electric switchboard. Fortunately it wasn't very badly damaged. The wood part blackened a bit, that's all. Someone had been monkeying with the main fuse-box. A piece of eighteen copper wire was where the ordinary lead fuse-wire ought to be.' Craig looked interested. The other nodded in the direction of the group Craig had just left. 'Caretaker chap swears the usual fuse-wire was in it three or four days ago. I don't know whether you know, but it's quite easy to create ignition by tampering with electric wiring.'

'Tell me,' Craig said.

'You scrape off the rubber insulating cover from the wire where it runs against any woodwork. You twist on a small coil of copper wire. That forms a resistance. It soon gets red hot and the woodwork catches fire. You have to make sure the circuit doesn't fuse, of course, so you substitute a piece of thick wire in the fuse-box.'

Craig caught on roughly. He queried:

'You think someone deliberately organised this flare-up?'

The other paused thoughtfully before replying.

'Only thing worrying me,' he said

slowly, 'is why the fuse-wire wasn't replaced in the fuse-box. You'd think, if someone did fix it the way I've been telling you, they'd cover up their traces afterwards.'

'Maybe this fuse-box fiddler was disturbed by the caretaker. Maybe something happened that made him forget.'

'That's what it looks like to me. My idea,' he said heavily, 'is this fire was criminally started by electrical ignition.'

Some time later Craig got back and was surprised to find Simone waiting for him. She put down the novel she was reading and he grinned as he saw it was a detective story. She mixed him a drink which suited him very well. His throat felt as if it were lined with cinders.

'A pal of yours 'phoned,' Simone said. 'Mr. Holt. Bill Holt. He said it was something you had asked him about Jeffrey Brook.'

Craig finished his drink and held out his glass.

'I could use that all over again. Jeffrey Brook doesn't mean a thing to me at this time of night.'

'He said it was important,' she told him as she got him another drink. 'He said he had been making inquiries from various people connected with some insurance company.'

'City Star?'

She nodded.

'City Star. He said there never was anyone on the staff of City Star named Jeffrey Brook.'

14

Not once did Jeffrey mention the woman in grey. During the rest of the day he grew more silent and reserved, and when he spoke his voice was harsh and nervy. It was as if he were suffering some inner conflict. The distant look in his eyes, as though he were watching something far away. The troubled lines on his forehead. It all added to his strange mood of silence. Sometimes he would smile suddenly, as if to reassure Helen there was nothing wrong.

But something was wrong, of that she was certain. If only he would confide in her. But she knew his fear, the inward anxiety, his nagging preoccupation with impending possibilities kept his mind away from hers. She was left alone, isolated.

Helen felt more calm now than during those few weeks before her marriage. She was stronger, more sure of herself now that she was his wife. She found she could view her problem more objectively. Again her thoughts turned to the meeting she had witnessed between Jeff and the blonde in the Piccadilly Circus tube station. The girl who was perhaps Lucy Evans. Had this meeting with her been an accident? She was going over old ground, she knew, but she might hit on something which would give her an answer to part of the problem. In any case she couldn't help herself. Perhaps the girl really was someone's secretary; someone he'd met in the course of the day's business and accidentally encountered again on that particular night.

Perhaps, she thought, she had been foolish to jump to conclusions. She had been over-anxious. All those times when he had 'phoned her saying business was keeping him from meeting her; all those anxious hours when she had waited for him; all those little explanations which he had given so glibly. Perhaps he had been telling her the truth. Perhaps she had worried needlessly, her anxiety distorted by her overactive imagination. Looking back, she wondered if Jeff's explanations for his actions were not, after all, perfectly reasonable.

Then what was it that was wrong with him? What was it upsetting the smooth routine of their life?

The woman in grey might have nothing to do with his silent preoccupation. But, on the other hand, her sudden appearance at the old house had obviously affected him. His watchful face was still fresh in her mind. She remembered how the muscles round his mouth had tightened, his eyes half closed. The way he had dismissed the strange woman with a casualness too assumed to be convincing.

Helen could not believe that Jeff's secret, whatever it was, was too serious for her to share. Perhaps it was just something that might interfere with his getting on in his business. People kept secrets for all sorts of stupid reasons, she knew, but somehow Jeff did not seem to be the sort of person to create a foolish misunderstanding over something trivial and easily explained.

She knew she must wait with patience

to find out what was in his mind. If only the thing, whatever it was, could be brought out into the open, she was sure she could help him cope with it. The evening of their visit to the old house, Helen had made an attempt, rashly, to persuade him to talk to her.

'Aren't you feeling a bit run down, Jeff?'

'I don't think so. Why do you ask?'

'I just thought you were looking a little tired.'

Then he had smiled that sudden smile.

'You're quite right, my dear. Forgive me if I seem irritable. I need a change of air. I shall be all right when we move out into the country.'

Helen knew instinctively she had tried too soon to bring to light his hidden thoughts. Time and tact and care were needed. Whatever his fear was, she must gradually win his confidence, show him his problems were hers, too.

She remembered that lovely day in Switzerland when they had sat overlooking Lucerne, the sun glittering on the water. A special understanding had sprung up between them like a kind of magic. It was an intimacy which she had longed to recapture.

Jeff started talking about the old house. Its name was Quarry Lodge. It seemed there was an old quarry nearby, now disused and overgrown. Jeff wanted to get into the house right away. He explained that the furniture was included in the sale. The previous owners had gone abroad to live and wanted to sell up the whole place. Thus the problems of moving in were considerably simplified. He seemed to have everything cut and dried. She realised he must have had the plan to move into the house at the back of his mind for some time.

The next day a servants' agency sent along several married couples. Jeff had fixed that up, too. Helen finally chose a pair named Mr. and Mrs. Langley.

Langley was a thin, elegant old butler character. Helen thought, with amusement, he had the perfect voice for saying: 'Dinner is served.' His wife was a large, heavy woman with a square face. She was obviously the practical type, with no nonsense about her, and she kept her husband well under her thumb.

'Mr. Brook says you'll be moving down there in a day or two,' she told Helen.

Disguising her surprise that it was to be as soon as that, Helen nodded.

'If that will be convenient?'

'Yes, madam.'

The following day Jeff and Helen left their flat for the last time. It was late afternoon and getting dusk as the car swung through the drive gates and up to the front door of Quarry House. She had not questioned Jeff's anxiety to move into their new home. If that was what he wanted, it must be that way. If the old house were going to make him happy, then she was determined to make it an ally on her side. With irresistible inward amusement, she realised she was acting as if she had been married to him for years.

15

The next morning Helen drove Jeffrey to catch his train to London. On her return, she decided to go for a walk while the sun was still out. A conference with Mrs. Langley, who had arrived with her husband early that morning, on the subject of food supplies could be postponed till later. She wanted to get out before the clouds crossed the sky and the sunshine faded.

She made her way to the thick belt of trees by the overgrown tennis court. The moss smelled rich and deep as she went in beneath the green of the trees. Patches of yellow sunlight streaked through the treetops. The sudden flutter of birds was the only sound. She was turning over in her mind the possibility of Jeffrey being in a confidential mood that evening. She wondered if it might be too soon for her to try and question him. The evening before she thought he had once seemed on the point of telling her something. But the moment had vanished and not returned. To-night, she decided, she would keep extra careful watch and give him every encouragement to speak.

She turned back the way she had come and, emerging from the trees, approached the house. She found it difficult to believe that it was theirs. Only a few days ago she had been looking forward to a new life at the flat without even knowing that the old house existed. And then Jeffrey's surprising news, his haste to move, his rushing her off her feet, the hurried packing, and here she was.

Mrs. Langley was waiting for her as she went into the house. Her square, grim face was impassive as she said:

'Have you a key to the room at the end of the top landing?'

Helen was surprised.

'But I gave you all the keys when you arrived.'

'All except this one, madam. The door is locked and I can't get in.'

Helen knew the room in question, but she had never been inside it. She had noticed before that it was locked. It looked now as if the key were missing.

'Could your husband do something about the lock?' she suggested.

'I'll ask him, madam.'

Helen turned at the sound of a car coming up the drive. A moment later it stopped outside and she glimpsed two men getting out. Langley appeared from nowhere and answered the bell. He followed Helen into the lounge.

'Dr. Foster,' he said. He coughed and added: 'And another gentleman with him.'

'What do they want? Who are they?'

'Dr. Foster asked if he could see you, madam. He didn't say what about.'

'All right,' Helen said. 'Ask them to come in.'

Dr. Foster was a thin little man, carefully dressed, while his companion was larger and almost burly.

'I hope you will forgive us for disturbing you,' Dr. Foster apologised. 'We are calling as a matter of routine at all the isolated houses in this district. I should explain that I am the doctor in

116

charge of the Woodland Nursing Home near here. This is Mr. Ratcliffe, a specialist in the treatment of nervous cases.' He paused. 'Woodlands,' he went on, 'is for want of a better word a — ah — mental home.'

'Lunatic asylum,' the big man said brusquely. 'Why not say so?'

Dr. Foster frowned, coughed and then continued.

'A most unfortunate incident occurred two days ago. One of the women patients managed somehow to leave the premises without being noticed. It really is most annoying. She was a very satisfactory case. She was making extremely good progress in every way. In a few months' time we should have succeeded in adjusting her equilibrium so that she would have been able to return to the outside world. She was really almost normal.'

'She was crackers,' the other man said.

Dr. Foster swung round angrily.

'Ratcliffe, kindly leave this to me. I especially don't want to alarm Mrs. Brook unnecessarily.' He turned back to

Helen and his voice was calm as he said: 'And I can assure you there *is* no cause for alarm, Mrs. Brook. The patient, though technically insane, is in no way dangerous.'

'Poor thing,' Helen murmured.

Dr. Foster nodded agreement.

'My object in coming here is to ask you if you would be good enough to telephone me immediately at the nursing home if you should happen to encounter the patient. Or, alternatively, get in touch with the local police station. The woman was seen in this vicinity yesterday by a farm-hand, but of course she may be anywhere now.'

Helen said: 'How should I recognise her?'

'She is a highly-strung type,' began the other before he was interrupted by the man called Ratcliffe, who growled:

'Woman of about fifty. Dressed all in grey.'

Helen was barely conscious of her two visitors leaving. She was dimly aware of the car starting up outside and driving off. Her thoughts were jumbled round the picture of the woman in grey as she had seen her a few mornings ago. Why had she come to Quarry House? Had she once lived here? Was she expecting to meet someone?

She was still in a maze of conjecture when Mrs. Langley came in.

'Shall I get my husband to take the lock off that door now, madam?'

Helen was still collecting her thoughts.

'What door?'

'On the top landing, madam. The one there isn't a key to.'

Helen said:

'Perhaps, after all, we had better wait until Mr. Brook comes back. He may have the key somewhere.'

'Very well, madam.'

Helen stood hesitating for some time. Then she made up her mind and went out of the room. The stairs creaked in the heavy silence as she went up to the musty top landing. She passed three rooms, the doors of which were open. It was the room at the end which was locked. There was no mistake about it. She turned the handle and pushed, but the door held firm. There was nothing to indicate why it should be locked. Perhaps there was no reason at all. Perhaps it was just that the key had been lost.

A horrible feeling of panic suddenly overcame her as she stood by the door. The atmosphere on the landing had suddenly become chilly. She became convinced that someone was watching her from one of the other rooms. She stood still, hardly daring to move. Her heart began thudding in her throat. She had to make a supreme effort before she could manage to run to the stairs. She expected every moment that some horrible hand would clutch at her shoulder. She almost fell down the stairs in her haste and then, recovering herself, she hurried down the next stairway to the hall, where she bumped, gasping, into Mrs. Langley.

'Whatever is the matter, madam?'

'Nothing. Nothing. I — do you think you could bring me a cup of tea, Mrs. Langley?'

'What you need, if I may say so, madam, is a nip of brandy in it. You look as if you've seen a ghost.'

Helen was determined not to let Mrs. Langley know how foolishly scared she had been.

'I'm perfectly all right,' she said, 'but I would love a cup of tea.'

16

When Jeffrey arrived that evening, Helen was waiting anxiously to talk to him. There were some logs blazing in the fire-place and she had some sherry ready on a small table. She had made up her mind to wait no longer. It was now or never. She watched him light a cigarette, and then, managing to keep the tone of her voice casual, she said:

'By the way, darling, some people called this morning.'

He took a sip at his sherry.

'Who?'

'It was a Dr. Foster and another man. They'd come from a nursing home near here.' She hesitated a moment, and then: 'A mental home.'

She felt rather than saw him stiffen suddenly. Lines appeared at the corner of his mouth and his eyes were looking down, avoiding hers. She asked:

'Do you know them?'

He shook his head.

'What did you say the name was?'

'Dr. Foster. It was the Woodland Mental Home.'

He gulped down the remainder of his sherry.

'What the devil did they want?' he queried, and his voice was harsh and taut.

She took the glass from him and caught his hand in hers. She looked straight into his eyes.

'Jeffrey, darling, why don't you tell me what it is? I know there's something on your mind. Every time you try to conceal it from me, it becomes plainer. You know this Dr. Foster, don't you? Why do you pretend to me that you don't?'

He looked away.

'You're talking nonsense, Helen,' he said over his shoulder.

But she knew his reserve was cracking. She must go on now. Only her determination could break through the defence he was throwing up. She mustn't give in.

'Don't be like this, Jeffrey. I'm your wife. You can trust me. Whatever it is, you don't have to be afraid to tell me. I want to know because I want to help you. If you love me, you won't keep me in this uncertainty.'

Still not looking at her, he said sharply: 'No need to be hysterical.'

She forced her mind to keep to its purpose. She refused to give in. Drawing a deep breath, she framed the question which had worried her ever since they had first come to view the house.

'Who was the woman in grey?'

Silence.

That was the only result her query had produced. Silence. Jeffrey got up and poured himself some more sherry. His hand was steady. Helen could see his mouth was set and uncompromising. He took a sip from the glass and eyed her over it.

'Listen to me,' he said slowly, quietly. 'I don't know this Dr. Foster and I haven't the slightest idea who this woman in grey is you're talking about. And if you imagine I'm suffering from some secret sorrow, get the idea right out of your head. It just happens I'm a little tired after working hard all day. That's all.'

He was slipping away from her after she had so nearly held him within her grasp. The atmosphere of confidence she had hoped to create was fast disappearing. She made another desperate effort to recapture that intimacy which had been between them only a few minutes before.

'You can't go on like this, Jeff. You can't go on hiding things from me. I'm not a fool. I've been noticing a lot about you for days. Ever since we were married. Before then. Jeff' — she spoke in whisper — 'there was a girl murdered in London a few days ago. Her picture was in the papers. Jeff did you know her?'

She had said it.

She had given voice to the tormenting thought at last. She was surprised she felt so calm about it. He tapped the ash off his cigarette unconcernedly. He looked at her with a little smile. But she knew it took all his strength to force that smile to his lips.

'You're being just a little ridiculous. What girl? I don't know any girl who's been murdered. Really, Helen, I can't understand this crazy idea you've got that

I'm keeping something from you.' He crossed over to the fire and stood staring into it. 'I'm afraid the conversation's beginning to bore me. I wish you'd change the subject.'

Helen fought to control herself. She wanted to beg him not to torture himself and her the way he was doing. She wanted to beg him not to hold out against her like this. But she knew it would be fatal if she made an exhibition of herself. That way would be the end of any further chances of gaining his confidence.

'I'm sorry,' she said calmly and began to search wildly in her mind for something else to talk about. 'By the way,' she went on, 'Mrs. Langley was asking about a key to-day. One of the rooms upstairs is locked. Have you got the key, by any chance?'

'What room?'

'At the end of the top landing.'

Thoughtfully he blew a cloud of cigarette-smoke before replying.

'What d'you want in there?'

She caught his tone and said:

'Nothing particularly, darling. I just

tried to get into it and couldn't. And Mrs. Langley wants the key.'

'I shouldn't bother about it. In any case, I gave you all the keys.' He turned away as if he'd dismissed the matter.

'Don't be silly,' she said. 'We must be able to get into the room when we want to. However, I'll get Langley to unscrew the lock.'

He turned on her suddenly, his face contorted. He ground through his teeth:

'I don't want that room opened. I forbid you, d'you understand? *No one must go into that room.*'

17

The telephone on Craig's desk suddenly jangled into life. He picked up the receiver and spoke into it.

'Morning, Nat,' Bill Holt's voice came to him over the wire.

'Hello, Bill. Thanks for ringing last night.'

'Okay. You asked me for the dirt on that factory in Shoreditch. The fire policies were taken out in the name of the South London Property Development Company, Victoria.'

'You're a real pal,' Craig told him.

'Glad to help you, Nat. Incidentally, I don't know if you're interested in that fire last night. The Elephant and Castle blaze.'

'Supposing I am?'

'The policies for that were also in the name of the South London Property Development Company.'

Craig said into the mouthpiece:

'What about the Park View Hotel, Richmond?'

'Park View Hotel was in the name of Riverside Hotels, Ltd. They were the people who owned the joint.'

Craig made a note of the name and hung up.

He got up and walked over to the window, staring down thoughtfully at the street. He lit a cigarette and went into the outer office. Lounging against the door, he scowled slightly at Simone.

'Do you not like my new lipstick?' she said and dived into her handbag for a mirror.

'You can stop worrying about that,' he told her. 'I was thinking about something quite different. Possibly a little more important, too.'

'A lipstick can be very important to a woman.'

He nodded.

'Let's not work ourselves into an acrimonious argument about that.'

'Let us not,' she agreed.

He continued to frown at her and then, after a moment, he asked slowly:

'Would you say I was gifted with a vivid imagination?'

'To stop you glaring at me like that, I would say anything.'

'I don't want my imagination to make a mug of me,' he said, 'but I've just had all the earmarks of a bright idea.'

'Tell me,' she encouraged him. 'Perhaps it will be a terrific idea.'

'My hunch is, there's a fire-bug organisation operating in London. What's more, our friend Jeffrey Brook is mixed up in it. Plus which, it ties in with that Maida Vale murder.'

Simone's eyes widened as he went on:

'Lucy Evans was secretary to a character named Anthony Webber. He is the brain behind the South London Property Development Company. The South London Property Development Company is the organisation owning the places that go up in smoke. Right now I don't quite see where Jeffrey Brook fits in, except he was playing around with Lucy Evans.'

'Are you going to tell me that Jeffrey Brook goes around setting fire to places and murdering people?'

He was silent for a moment. Then, ignoring her question, he said:

'This morning I checked through the file of a case I handled before you gave this place tone by coming to work for me. The Nicholas Rice job, it was. Rice was another of those smart brains who saw a chance of making easy money. He was an insurance assessor and, no doubt, he worried the idea for quite a time while he was going about his ordinary business. One day he met a character named Jepson. This Jepson owned a wholesale fabric firm in North London. Rice made the suggestion he should insure the business for as much as possible, then burn it down and claim the insurance. Jepson wasn't doing so well, so he agreed to this bright little scheme. The best bales of fabric were removed from the ware-house and the place was set alight.'

'But how did this Jepson set fire to the place without it looking suspicious?' Simone asked.

'He had an ingenious system which provided him not only with the fire,'

Craig told her, 'but also with an alibi. It went this way: a lighted candle was placed in a wastepaper basket full of shavings. Several hours elapsed until the candle burned down to the shavings. By the time the place went up in flames Mr. Jepson had established an alibi miles away. Nicholas Rice was careful enough to have no connection with the business. In fact, he'd provided most of the money to buy the insurance and he took a very nice cut of the proceeds.'

Craig took a deep drag at his cigarette and continued:

'It began to look to Rice as if he'd got quite a cosy idea. He went to work to find another buddy who was willing to come in on a similar proposition. This stooge owned the same type of business the other side of London. Adams, his name was. The premises, after being very much over-insured, also went up in smoke with Jepson doing the job again. From now on, Mr. J. became Rice's trusty fire-bug.'

'What an extraordinary business,' Simon breathed.

Craig shrugged.

'It's one way of earning a living, if you feel you must earn your living that way. Anyway, Rice now decided to go in for it in a big way. He picked two or three more pals to give him a hand and their next job was a firm in the city. The stock inside the place was removed just before the fire, though the insurance claim made afterwards naturally included this. Plus which, fake invoices showed much more stuff than was ever on the premises. Rice was able to make everything look nice and legal by dumping partly burnt stock in the place afterwards. He cleaned up very nicely over this and looked around for the next one. And so began a row of fires.'

'When was this Mr. Rice found out?'

'One of the insurance firms involved decided that they were paying out too much in fire claims and began wondering. They called yours truly in and I started to dig around. Believe me, there was plenty to dig into at that.

'Rice worked his racket the same way every time. He found a firm that wasn't making the grade, he approached them discreetly. The firm agreed to the insurance and the burning down. And every time Mr. Jepson did the job. I came in just about the time when a chap in one of these firms thought his share of the cash wasn't enough. He tried putting the black on Jepson. Jepson came to me, spilled some of the dirt, and that was that.'

Simone nodded and said:

'It's all very interesting. But I do not quite see what it has to do with Jeffrey Brook.'

'Last night a silk-goods warehouse down by the Elephant and Castle was burnt out,' Craig told her. 'I'm tipped off someone had fixed the fuse in the way someone would fix a fuse if they wanted to start a fire by an electrical leakage. I am also tipped off that this silk-goods warehouse is owned by the South London Property Development Company.' Craig paused to flick ash off his cigarette.

'A little while back,' he continued, 'a carton factory in Shoreditch went up in smoke. By a curious coincidence it was owned by the South London Property Development Company. Some time before then an hotel had caught fire at Richmond and, though I can't as yet tie it up with the South London Property Development people, it doesn't necessarily let them out.'

'In other words — ' Simone began.

'In other words,' Craig said grimly, 'I have a hunch someone has taken a leaf out of Nicholas Rice's book.'

Simone gave a sudden exclamation.

'The South London Property Development Company — that is where that girl worked.'

Craig nodded.

'You see how the thing is beginning to add up. Lucy Evans used to work at the dump and along comes this Jeffrey Brook, who was in the insurance business himself, and he runs around with the girl.'

Simone nodded thoughtfully.

'Poor Helen. It will be ghastly for her.'

'It wasn't so funny for Lucy Evans. Let's go over some of that old ground again,' he went on, 'just to double-check. The unfinished letter found in her room which she'd been writing to her boy-friend. In it she began by saying she was crazy over him, then she changed her tune. She threatened to send him up the river because she'd got the goods on him. That was if he tried any funny business like leaving her flat. Then the way she'd been interrupted by the boy-friend and had thrown the letter away. Next little item: the coat button which had been torn off, presumably in a struggle. And this Jeffrey Brook coming back after his so-called business appointment with a button missing from his coat.'

'A little circumstantial,' Simone interrupted him, 'but Jeffrey Brook might have been in the dead girl's room.'

'I'll settle for that for now,' Craig agreed, 'which brings me back to the firm at Victoria and the pert little switchboard number who tipped me off Lucy Evans had been running around with a character from Pyramid Assurance.'

Simone nodded slowly.

'Let us say then,' she said, 'that Jeffrey Brook was the girl's boy-friend.'

'I've already said it,' Craig reminded her, grinning bleakly, 'and I know more than that about him. I know that he got himself a job with Pyramid Assurance by fixing himself up with a phoney letter of introduction from another company that went smash. And just to make it a nice round sum, you can add to it that evening at the Café Rouge, when he pushed off to keep a business appointment around the same time Lucy Evans died.'

'I wonder,' Simone mused, 'if I ought to telephone Helen and see if she is all right? You do not think — ?

She broke off, alarm shadowing her face. He shook his head.

'I'd let that ride. So long as she knows nothing, she'll be all right.'

'I could just 'phone her casually,' Simone suggested.

'Make it cagey,' he warned her. 'Don't let her suspect you know anything. For her own sake.'

He went back into his office.

A little later Simone came in. She was looking slightly worried.

'I have been talking to Helen,' she said. 'They have given up their flat. They have moved into a house in the country.'

Craig eyed her with a frown.

'Big time, eh?'

'I rang up the flat,' Simone explained.

'Someone else has taken it over. They told me where Helen was and I got on to her.'

'How did she sound?'

'She sounded all right,' Simone said. 'But there is something funny about it. She said Jeffrey had been left some money and had bought the house on the spur of the moment. She had been run off her feet, she said. It is an old house down in Buckinghamshire. She asked to be remembered to you.'

Craig nodded. He didn't say anything for a moment, but watched a smoke-ring drift lazily up from his cigarette. Presently he murmured:

'So some rich someone's left Jeffrey Brook a slab of money and he's moved out of town to live. It sounds very nice. I wish some rich someone would leave me a slab of money and I'd get the hell out, too.' He shook his head. 'It reeks,' he said. 'The whole set-up reeks any way you slice it.'

18

I

The girl with the tip-tilted nose looked up as Craig came over to the switchboard and gave him a dazzling smile.

'This is nice,' she said.

'Me, too,' Craig told her and then glanced sharply over her shoulder at the door with 'Anthony Webber' on the frosted glass. The door was slightly open. The voices of two people could be heard plainly within. Craig recognised one voice as Webber's. The other belonged to a woman and she sounded pretty temperamental.

'If you think you can treat me the way you treat all the rest of them, you've made a big mistake.'

'For God's sake, Dolores, not here. I'll 'phone you to-night and we'll talk this over.'

Suddenly the door slammed shut.

Presumably Webber had discovered it was open and hadn't been pleased by the realisation.

Craig turned back to the girl with an eyebrow lifted quizzically. He was about to offer some comment when Webber's door was suddenly swung open and the woman he'd called Dolores came out, heading for the exit. She didn't glance to right or left. Craig took a good look at her as she went past, and, whichever way he considered it, he wasn't wasting his time. She was a tall, dark and curvacious type. She was exquisitely dressed and a cloud of exotic perfume trailed after her.

'Who would that be?' Graig asked.

'The Queen of Sheba,' the girl said shortly.

She sounded envious and Craig gave her a grin. He glanced over at Webber's door. It was closed. To the girl at the switchboard he said.

'Hungry?'

'What for? Love?'

'Lunch.'

'That's different. I'm supposed to be meeting someone.'

'Couldn't you duck him for once?'

She smiled at him.

'How do you know it's a him?'

'You forget, I'm a detective.'

She regarded him for a moment, her head on one side.

'Okay,' she said. 'Wait for me outside.'

A few minutes later she joined him in the street She was wearing a smart little suit and an air of superb self-confidence. She took his arm in a proprietory manner.

'Where are we going, darling? The Ritz?'

'For you and me, somewhere a little more intimate,' he said.

'I'm going to enjoy every minute of this, I can see.'

They got into a taxi and Craig gave the name of a little restaurant off Greek Street. It was a smartly got-up place and currently enjoyed a fashionable clientele. The tubby, smooth-faced *maître d'hôtel* came bobbing forward at Craig's appearance.

'Good morning, Mr. Craig. Good morning, madam.'

He found them a table tucked away in a corner. The girl glanced round, taking it all in. She smiled across the table at him.

'I love this,' she said. She started asking him the names of various people at other tables. Presently Craig got her to talk about herself. Her name was Rita Spear. She was twenty and she was going around with a boy called Len who was sincere but sloppy. Len wanted to marry her and sometimes she wanted to marry him. But not all the times.

Over coffee he began talking about Lucy Evans. Rita's nose became slightly more *retroussé* and she said couldn't they talk about something more thrilling? Couldn't they talk about him and what it was like being a private detective. He told her being a private detective was like hell, except when there was an attractive stooge around who could help him crack the case. She said he knew all the answers and, all right, he only had to ask her what he wanted to know about Lucy and little Rita would tell him what she could.

'For a start, can you remember roughly the date the character from the Pyramid

Assurance first dropped in?'

She thought for a moment.

'I'd say it was about five weeks ago, but I can't give you the exact date.'

'Was he a stranger, or had he called on Webber at any time before?'

She shook her head.

'I don't remember him before.'

'So you'd say it's unlikely he was a pal of Webber?'

'I don't think they knew each other. He just came about some insurance. We do a lot of insuring, you know. Mr. Webber buys properties and sometimes they stay on our hands for quite a long time. Naturally we have them insured against fire. He just came about some fire insurance.'

Craig eyed her through a cloud of cigarette-smoke. Her expression was innocent enough. He decided she didn't know a thing more than she was telling him. He said:

'So he looks in to arrange for some insurance and goes for Lucy in a big way first time he spots her?'

'Right.'

'That was about five weeks ago. And since then she'd been going around with him pretty steadily until she was bumped off?'

She nodded.

'Would Webber know anything about her and this chap?'

'I'm not Mr. Webber's girl-friend, you know,' she told him. 'He's not my type. So I can't say what he knows and what he doesn't know. Though I'd imagine that even if I were his girl-friend, he wouldn't tell me much about the office. He's the sort who keep their thoughts to themselves. A bit crafty, I'd say.' She added, irrelevantly: 'I wish I was crafty. Perhaps I'll try it one day. I might make something out of it.' A speculative look hovered in her eyes for a moment. Then she said suddenly: 'You're not going to tell me he had anything to do with the murder? That he and Lucy were having a secret affair and he did her in because he was jealous of this other chap?'

His smile was enigmatic. He said:

'How about the dark piece who was in his office this morning?'

144

'Oh, her. Temperamental, isn't she? She's an actress, or something.' She put any amount of meaning into it. 'Dolores Brant, she calls herself. If you ask me, she's one of his mistakes. She's got her hooks into him and the poor fish is wriggling.'

'Too bad.'

'Always sending her flowers, he was once. I used to have to ring up for them every morning. Dozen white carnations one day. Orchids the next. Roses. Her flat must have looked like a flower-show.'

'Where'd she live? Remember?'

She bit her lower lip so that the lipstick came off on her small white teeth.

'Tower Court, Bayswater. I don't seem to remember the number.'

'She still live there?'

She nodded.

'Why? You going to do something about it?'

'Maybe I could call you up sometime and let you know.'

She eyed him for a moment, head a little on one side, her expression suddenly enigmatic. Or was it faintly mocking? She might be thinking anything and probably was. He found himself starting in to wonder what went on inside that head, what was it made her tick. She was saying:

'I like being with you. I like the way you talk. It's as good as the movies.'

In the taxi on the way back to the South London Development Offices she turned to him as if on a sudden impulse.

'Could I call at where I live on the way?'

'Where d'you live?'

She gave him the address and he told the driver. 'I've got a room in my cousin's flat,' she said. 'She's married, her husband's away all the week.' She threw him an oblique glance and added: 'I do believe my cousin's out this afternoon, too.'

His gaze flickered over her. He only said:

'Will I be safe, alone with you?'

'Who says I'm inviting you in?'

'I was too quick,' he grinned at her.

She laughed and held on to his arm. When the taxi pulled up outside a small block of flats behind St. Martin's Lane she said to him to tell the driver not to wait. He started to say something, but she turned and hurried into the flats. He stood staring after her for a few moments. Then he paid off the driver.

The flat was small and shabby. Except her room. To his surprise, it was furnished with evident care, it was curiously restful. He'd expected it to be cluttered with pictures of film-stars and the rest. Instead there was one picture on the cream-painted walls: a reproduction of something by someone.

'Like it?' she asked as he took in the room.

'Cosy.'

She smiled at him, pleased, and snapped on the radio.

'Should be some sloppy dance-music.'

Instead there was a voice on bird-sanctuaries. She made a wry face at him and fiddled with the dial. She got an orchestra playing treacly afternoon-music.

'It'll do.'

'For who?'

'You and me.'

For the first time she stood and looked at him squarely. He stared back at her. There was a curious tenseness about her. He realised with a sense of shock it was just as if she were gnawed with hunger. It was just as if she were burning up with it. He could see little beads of perspiration on her upper lip. Deliberately he took out his cigarette-case.

'Light me one,' she said. Her voice was low, harsh.

He lit a cigarette and gave it her. Her fingers shook as she took it from him. Then she dragged at it long and luxuriously. Then she turned away with a quick movement and was looking out of the window.

'What happens to your job?' he asked the back of her neck. 'If you don't turn up this afternoon?'

'I'll 'phone presently and say I was taken ill at lunch. There's a girl who can take over for me this afternoon.'

'Got it all worked out.'

'It's being with you, you give me ideas.' She turned back to him. 'Besides, I can come and work for you. It must be fun working for a detective.'

'Remind me to tell my secretary that.'

She asked the obvious question:

'Is she pretty?'

'She's a good secretary, too.'

She moved quickly and drew the curtains together. In the sudden gloom her face as she moved to him was pink above her cigarette. The cigarette-glow came nearer to him. She was looking up into his face and she took her cigarette and stubbed it out. Her eyes were shining in the whiteness of her face. Her hand reached up and took his cigarette and stubbed it out besides hers.

He said:

'What will Len say?'

'He'll never get the opportunity of knowing,' she said enigmatically. 'And what he doesn't know he won't get all jealous over. You think I'm acting like any tart, don't you? So go ahead and think it. I'm just crazy over you, that's all it is.'

'You want to go through all this to prove it?'

'How else? You expect me to write you a letter about it?'

He didn't answer her. He just stared at her, his eyes suddenly speculative.

'What's the matter?' she said. 'You like me, don't you?'

'You're a sweet kid.'

'You wait one day when I've got some money. When I'm all organised like these women you see. Clothes, hair-do, facial, I'll have you falling over yourself for me then. You don't know how I'd like to look like that for you.'

'You look fine to me now,' he said.

'In this light,' she laughed at him. Her eyes were wide, dark and shining. Her mouth was slightly open and glistening. He could see the glimmer of her teeth. The scent of her hair was nice, he liked it. He could feel the warmth of her. A sudden stab of pity for her sharp with a poignancy he couldn't explain dug deep into him. She was another one searching pathetically for something she couldn't put a name to. In his own way he was the same himself. He was looking for something he didn't know what, letting life kick him around, being smart and tough just to give himself a living. He didn't flatter himself she was just yearning for him. It was a longing that went deeper, deeper than she could know. She was like him and a million million others seeking wildly, futilely some illumining flash that would show through the tawdriness and shabbiness of existence that other something that should be beautiful. The end of the rainbow, if you like. And all she could find to help her look was the stuff that was churned out in glossy magazines or projected on a screen in the lonely darkness that blurred the other seekers all around her. She wouldn't find any part of it the way she was going about it, but who was to help her?

Did he have the key? He who was in the same spot himself, except that from where he was standing it looked a little different. He who was just another solitary so-and-so grubbing around, hiring himself out to clients who were so dumb or so scared they didn't know when to come in out of the rain. He who was cluttering up his days and nights with sudden death and dreary chicanery that he didn't want any part of. He who only wanted to coast his way along like any human being was meant to. He wondered if maybe getting religion wouldn't be the only way out for him.

'I think you're afraid of me,' she said and he brought his thoughts back to her again.

'Scared stiff.'

He was at the door.

'Aren't you — ? Don't you want to stay?' she said.

'I told you,' he said, smiling at her slowly. 'You frighten me.'

There was a little pause, while she stared at him sulkily. 'All right,' she muttered, 'if that's the way it is.'

He nodded. He said:

'I won't forget to call you.'

'I can hardly wait,' she threw at him. But the door had already closed on him.

II

Tower Court had originally been a private house of four storeys before it had been converted and fitted with a small lift. It was one of those lifts operated by pulling hard on a rope and hoping something stops it before it goes through the roof. Craig found the contraption more or less in the charge of an ancient caretaker, who operated the thing when he wasn't drowsing in his cubby-hole or working out his racing prospects in the sports pages.

'Which floor is Miss Brant?'

The other disentangled a blackened briar from a gigantic walrus moustache. He regarded Craig sleepily.

'Second floor. Number ten. Arf a mo'. Would you be Mr. Webber?'

Webber.

Craig hesitated a bare second before he inclined his head.

'Miss Brant left a message for you. She's gone out and may not be back. She says, will you see her to-night after the show at the club. Important, she said.'

'What club?'

Craig supposed he ought to know, but he risked it, hoping it wouldn't make the caretaker suspicious. The old chap sucked uneasily at his pipe.

'The club where she's performing at, of course.'

Craig tried to will him to supply the name, but either the caretaker didn't know, or wasn't in the mood to be willed. His moustache drooped over his pipe again and he turned away.

Craig said:

'Wonder if Miss Brant has gone along there to rehearse?'

There was a disinterested grunt in reply.

Craig said:

'The number just escapes me. Got a 'phonebook?'

'Made a note of it meself somewhere,' the caretaker muttered and ducked into his cubby-hole. He reappeared in a moment, squinting short-sightedly at a piece of paper. 'Be on that, only I can't make it out.'

Among a collection of pencilled hiero-glyphics Craig picked out:

'Miss Brant, Gardenia Club, Piccadilly 8150.'

As the grubby talons closed over the

paper again, Craig caught the sound of a taxi drawing up outside. A man got out and began diving into his pocket for some change. Craig recognised him as Anthony Webber.

Craig moved fast and gained the street, timing it so that he passed Webber while the other's back was turned to him as he paid off the driver. Craig felt pretty confident he hadn't been spotted as he walked quickly away.

19

I

It was six o'clock and the offices of the *Globe* were filled with a deep rumbling roar coming from the great rotary presses in the basement. The evening routine was in full swing. The business of making up the newspaper proceeded briskly and methodically, according to plan. The early pages of the first edition were taking shape. And over all this feverish activity time ruled. Time, measured minute by minute on the electric clocks in every room in the giant building.

Amongst the news coming in by telephone, cable and radio from all parts of the world was a call from a reporter at the Scotland Yard Press Bureau. He was 'phoning through the latest police bulletin.

Investigations on the Maida Vale murder mystery were proceeding satisfactorily in the hands of Detective-Inspector

Marraby. The latest developments had placed a further clue in the Inspector's possession. A taxi-driver had been found who remembered picking up a fare in the neighbourhood of Vale Crescent on the evening of the crime at about eight o'clock. The taxi-driver described his fare as being a man medium to tall in height. He thought he was youngish and well-built, wearing a hat but no overcoat. He had seemed excited and somewhat out of breath, the taxi-driver said, and had been driven to Baker Street Station.

That was all from the reporter at Scotland Yard Press Bureau.

II

Life at Number 5, Vale Crescent, had settled back into its uneventful pattern. Already the morbid excitement over Lucy Evans' murder was being forgotten. The occupants of Number 5 proceeded along their respective ways as before.

The landlady admitted to herself that she was beginning to regret the return of normality to her house. Murder had brought a decided spice, a thrill to the dreary round of existence. She glanced up at the newspaper enlargement of Lucy's photo which she had carefully cut out, framed and placed in a place of honour on the mantelpiece. She crossed over to the dresser, rummaged at the back of a drawer and took out a collection of clippings she had snipped from the *Globe*.

As she noisily sipped her tea, laced with a dash of rum, she pored over the accounts of the case again, reliving the incidents of that night. It was only when she caught footsteps in the hall overhead that she paused in her reading and looked up, a lascivious expression crossing her face.

Quietly she hurried to the foot of the stairs and, stealthily ascending as far as she dare, stood in the semi-darkness listening to the mutterings and gigglings of the girls and their visitors. She enjoyed the giggling the best of all. It caused the smile on her face to reach from ear to ear.

Miss Duveen paused at the long, narrow and somewhat spotted mirror by her door. She tilted the table-lamp so she could get a final look at herself before she went out.

Turning on her high heels, she peered over her shoulder at herself. She bent and carefully adjusted the seam in her stocking. She regarded her reflection critically. It was a new dark suit and it fitted her very nicely. She leaned forward to make sure she hadn't smudged her lipstick, then she stood back, turning slowly and looking at her legs. She was grateful for her legs. She had reason to be.

Miss Duveen gave her room a glance round and sighed a little and began dreaming again of the day when she would have a flat with a front door all to herself. She turned the door-handle, switched off the lamp and went out. She hurried past the room that had once been Lucy's. The room was still empty, though the landlady told Miss Duveen she hoped a new tenant would be taking it on next week. She shuddered involuntarily as she went by, the memory of that ghastly evening flooding back. Determinedly she pushed the horrible picture away from her mind and ran down the stairs.

The front door slammed and the clatter of Miss Duveen's high heels on the pavement receded and died away.

IV

As the front door slammed, another door opened and a girl looked out. She pulled her dressing-gown round her and brushed a piece of yellow hair from her eyes. She was smiling to herself as if still amused by something.

A man's voice spoke behind her and she turned.

'It was only that Miss Duveen going out, ducks. Don't be so nervous.'

The man in the room spoke again and she giggled and closed the door.

The frowsy, unshaven man downstairs had also heard the front door slam. It was as if he had been awaiting a signal. He threw a surreptitious glance at his wife, stood up and edged towards the door. She didn't look up from her darning.

He coughed hesitantly.

'Think I'll just pop out for a breath of air,' he said, reaching for his hat.

No answer.

'I won't be long, my dear.'

He swallowed noisily and opened the door, watching her carefully. Still she didn't say anything, didn't look up at him. He gave another spasmodic gulp and went out, closing the door behind him quickly. The woman bent over her darning heard his footsteps scuffling down the hall. She smiled sourly to herself.

Dirty-minded little rat, she thought unemotionally. As if he'd get anywhere with that flashy Miss Duveen.

V

The girl slipped into the 'phone-box and dialled. Now her heart was pounding in her throat so painfully she thought she wouldn't be able to speak. She was trembling all over and for a moment she felt she couldn't go through with it. Then she took a grip of herself.

The receiver was lifted at the other end. 'Hello?'

His voice sounded cautious and, in answer to her question, he paused before admitting his identity. She told him who she was and smiled as she pictured the look of puzzled surprise that must be on his face. She was feeling calm now. She decided she was beginning to enjoy the whole idea. She would make him look even more surprised before she was through.

'I'm speaking from Marble Arch,' she said. 'I think it would be a good idea if you came along right away and met me — '

'What the devil — ?'

But she went on quickly and firmly. 'I thought we might have a little chat about Lucy Evans. Remember her? The girl who was strangled. And you and I know who did it, don't we? That's what I would like

162

to talk to you about. The fact that you — *and I* — know.'

She paused, waiting for him to say something. For a second she thought the line was dead, that he had rung off. Then she could hear his breathing.

'Are you listening?' she asked and her tone was quite pert.

'I'm listening.'

'I'm glad you're interested. It would have been a pity if you'd hung up on me and I'd have had to go to the police.'

'What do you want?' he asked.

'A little chat with you. I'll be waiting in the main entrance of the Regal Hotel and I'll give you twenty minutes. I don't wait after that. We can find a quiet corner and have a drink. How does that suit? It suits me all right.'

'At the Regal Hotel in twenty minutes.'

'Main entrance and don't be late.'

He hung up.

She went out of the 'phone-box. She drew a deep breath. Well, she'd done it. Just like the movies. She'd always known she'd got the guts to live the way they did on the movies. She smiled defiantly and stuck out her lower lip. As she made her way into the crowded foyer of the Regal Hotel, she turned over in her mind the amount she should ask for.

Five hundred?

A thousand?

Better go easy to start with, she thought. Five hundred for the first go off. She could see how things went afterwards.

VI

The man at the wide desk replaced the receiver and sat for a moment staring at it unseeingly.

Still absorbed in his thoughts, he reached for a cigarette from the box in front of him. He tapped it automatically on the desk-edge and lit it. For several moments he drew at it nervously. Then he seemed to come to a decision. He glanced at his watch. He reached for the telephone again and dialled. After a moment:

'Hello? Speaking.' He kept his voice

very low. 'Something's gone wrong. Someone's found out more than is good for us. Yes, it's a girl. I think she's going to be very, very difficult.'

He listened to the voice at the other end, idly watching the smoke-rings from his cigarette. Then, in answer to a question, he said:

'She must be crazy, of course, to think she'll get away with it.'

Again he paused to listen to the other voice. Then:

'She's waiting at the Regal Hotel. Main entrance. She said she would give me twenty minutes.' A chill smile touched his mouth. He answered the two or three questions the other asked him and then rang off.

He cradled the receiver and began humming a little tune to himself.

VII

Gabriel Warwick walked out of the offices of Pyramid Assurance and, saluting him, the commissionaire raised his hand to bring a cruising taxi to the kerb.

Gabriel Warwick was about to step into the taxi when he heard footsteps behind him and turned. A good-looking young man was hurrying out of the building.

'Hello, Brook.'

Jeffrey Brook pulled up somewhat reluctantly. The other gave him a curious look. He said:

'You seem in a hurry. Can I give you a lift? Which way are you going?'

Jeffrey Brook hesitated. Then he muttered:

'Er — Paddington. Yes, I'm in rather a rush. Train to catch.'

'Ah, yes. You're living in the country now. I'm going part of the way. Hop in.'

'It's very kind of you — ' Jeffrey Brook began, glancing about a little wildly, 'but I think as I am rushing I'd better grab a taxi for myself.' He waved suddenly and shouted, and another taxi swung to the kerb. 'Thanks, all the same,' he called out as he quickly scrambled in. The taxi drew off with him.

Gabriel Warwick leaned back, staring ahead of him. He was frowning a little.

166

'Where to, sir?'

The driver's query jarred him out of his ruminations. He gave the address and the taxi drove away.

VIII

It was eighteen minutes by the clock over the reception desk across the crowded, bustling vestibule.

Another couple of minutes and she would know if her bluff had come off. She stood, jostled by the mob milling around her and kept her gaze fixed on the revolving door. The faces of the people coming into the hotel all reflected the pinkish-gold glow caused by the lighting. The hum of voices beat against her ear-drums like surf breaking on a beach, and every now and then she caught the murmur of the orchestra from the restaurant.

At moments she felt she was dreaming the whole thing. The pinkish golden faces drifting past her, the hum of conversation and the snatches of saccharine music, together with the reason for her being here, all added to the dream-like effect.

And then a voice was saying her name in her ear.

She spun round with a gasp. The man who was smiling at her wasn't the one she was expecting. She threw a glance over her shoulder towards the revolving doors. He followed her look. He took her arm. His grip was friendly, but firm.

'I'm afraid he won't turn up. I've come in his place.'

'You? But — ?'

'The name is Marraby. Detective-Inspector Marraby of Scotland Yard.'

She gazed at him, a chill closing over her. Her mouth opened and closed soundlessly. She remembered reading in the newspapers that he was in charge of the Maida Vale murder. So the swine had gone to the police, had he? The mean, dirty swine. They'd send her to prison.

Prison.

He interrupted her as she started to speak.

'Better not say anything now. Just come

168

along with me and we'll look in at the nearest police station. Just round the corner.'

He was impelling her towards an exit on the other side of the vestibule. His tone was conversational, almost casual. They might have been lovers meeting and going out for the evening.

So this was what being arrested was like.

They didn't do it this way on the films. The grip on her arm grew firmer as they pushed through the crowd. The realisation of the consequences of her folly hit her with all its force.

Stupid, mad little fool.

She must have been out of her senses to think she could have got away with bluffing him of all people.

'I didn't mean it, I didn't really,' she managed to choke as they reached the street.

He didn't answer. Merely urged her along the darkening side-street. She glanced at his face as she hurried beside him. It wasn't a bit like a Scotland Yard detective's face, she thought.

She pleaded:

'I was bluffing him, you see. I didn't really know anything about him and Lucy Evans. I was guessing, that's all. I thought I might frighten him into thinking I knew more than I did. I thought I might scare him I'd go to the police and involve him. It was just an idea to get a few pairs of silk stockings out of him.'

Still no reply.

She went on talking, some of her courage returning. It was her first offence. She'd never done anything like this before. It wasn't as if she were a real blackmailer. She had only been bluffing.

They turned into an opening sloping down to a mews, shadowed in the gathering dusk. She glimpsed a street-lamp glimmering on the corner at the other end of the cobbled yard.

'The police station's in the next street,' he murmured, his voice still friendly, almost gentle in her ear. Her pointed heels clattered on the cobble-stones.

She was still pleading animatedly as he halted suddenly, his face looming above hers. And now his face was changed. Now she knew a terror that stopped her heart.

'You're — you're not a — ' she began. And then his hands were pressing inexorably into her throat.

IX

The *Globe's* man covering the Scotland Yard Press Bureau came through to the news-room at about seven-thirty.

A young girl, pretty, had just been found in a mews behind the Regal Hotel. Strangled. Circumstances of the crime suggested that the Maida Vale murderer might be responsible for this latest killing. It was probably for this reason that Detective Inspector Marraby, who was conducting the investigations into the Lucy Evans case, had at once taken over inquiries into this fresh murder.

The victim had so far not been identified.

They got on to Craig and asked him if he thought it might be worth his while looking into it. He said he had had quite a tiring day and he didn't imagine how the murder of a girl in some mews could mean a thing in his life.

After he'd hung up, something made him change his mind and he went along to the mortuary where the girl had been taken.

20

When Craig got back, Simone started to tell him something. She broke off as she saw his face.

'What happened?'

'Rita Spear,' he told her, his voice flat. She gave a little gasp.

'Poor thing. To do with the other murder, do you think?'

He shrugged and took a cigarette from his case. He was pacing up and down and he paused to light the cigarette. Then he continued his restless pacing again. Simone realised that this second murder had shocked even his sensibilities, toughened as they had become by day-to-day encounters with the sordid and seamy, which were a part of his profession. He said:

'Marraby's taking care of it. He thinks the two tie up.'

'But why Rita Spear?'

'I've been asking myself that, plenty.

Either she knew more than she told me, or he thought she knew more than she did.'

'He?'

'The character who fixed her.'

'Jeffrey Brook?'

He exhaled slowly before replying. Then he nodded.

'It's a nag of that colour I've got my shirt on. At the moment.' He went on thoughtfully: 'Or maybe Rita acted the smart girl. Maybe she didn't know anything more than she spilled to-day. But I may have put ideas into her head.'

'You mean she may have gone to — to this man and tried to get money out of him?'

'It's just an idea I have.'

She shuddered. There was a little silence. Then she said:

'I started to tell you, the Professor's back.'

He stared at her over his cigarette.

'I stuck him into the outer office,' she said. 'He refused to go until he had seen you.'

Craig raised his eyes despairingly.

'You're a pal.'

'I am sorry,' she said. 'He insisted.'

The Professor was still wearing the filthy old mackintosh and, wound round his neck, was a scarf that looked like a moth-eaten boa-constrictor. His eyes lit up eagerly over his dark glasses.

'Good evening, Mr. Craig.'

'The office is shut.'

The other ignored Craig's acerbity and began:

'I came to see you the other day to offer my aid in solving the Maida Vale murder mystery.'

'I remember.'

'I must confess I am somewhat surprised not to have received any communication from you having regard to the important and far-reaching discovery I made.'

Craig was only half listening to him, but he said:

'I haven't had a chance of doing anything about it yet.'

'Never mind. Never mind,' the Professor told him magnanimously. 'I've brought you the chart I told you about.'

'Chart?'

The other's bald dome nodded with jerky enthusiasm.

'I have been through the records at the British Museum and I have compiled this chart showing how many murders during the last thirty years have taken place at the full moon.'

He produced a half-sheet of heavy cartridge-paper and unfolded it to display a complicated net-work of lines and dates and names. He went on impressively:

'All the murders in the last thirty years.' He jabbed a dirty forefinger. 'And this shows you when the moon was at the full.'

'Interesting, very interesting.'

'I am glad you think so,' the Professor said fervently, 'because this is what I am about to suggest.'

'Tell me.'

'I am going to suggest that your newspaper reproduces this chart on the front page to-morrow. And, of course, I should be fully prepared to contribute an article explaining how the identity of the murderer could be proved by these astrological and numerological conclusions.'

'That's remarkably generous of you.'

'Not at all, not at all.'

'But there's a possibility,' Craig went on, 'that the *Globe* might not see eye to eye with your proposal.'

'But, Mr. Craig. I don't think you quite understand. My chart would prove of inestimable value in the prevention of crime — '

'I absolutely agree,' Craig interrupted him. 'But my advice is for you to send it to Detective-Inspector Marraby of Scotland Yard.'

'You mean the officer in charge of the investigations of the Maida Vale mystery?'

'That's it.'

The Professor's eyes blinked doubtfully behind his spectacles.

'You are of the opinion that would be a good idea?'

'Marraby would love it,' Craig told him. 'Just his cup of tea.'

The other rolled up his precious paper and pushed it into his pocket.

'It's very good of you, Mr. Craig. I am most grateful.'

'Think nothing of it.'

'Good night, Mr. Craig. Good night.'

Craig closed the door after the greasy mackintosh and went and poured himself a stiff drink.

Around ten o'clock he was slipping into his double-breasted dinner-jacket. He gave a final tug to his tie and Simone, who had been touching up her mouth in his mirror, turned to regard him, eyes sparkling with approval.

'It will be good for you to be gay. It is gay? I have not been to the Gardenia before.'

'Just another dump,' he told her.

As they went down to the street the telephone started ringing. But they didn't hear it.

21

A brassy dance orchestra, with a lot of trumpet in it, was playing as they reached the crowded room well below street level. Skirting the edge of the small dance floor, they followed the waiter to a table. As they sat down, a putty-faced individual came over to them, smiling expansively and rubbing his fat hands together.

'I always say the very best people come to my club,' He bowed extravagantly to Simone. 'Good evening, madam. I am charmed to see you here. You will have a drink with me, of course.'

'You are very kind.' Simone was a little taken aback by all this flamboyance.

'He'll stick it on the bill, so don't look too gratified,' Craig told her.

The other laughed loudly and patted Craig on the shoulder. To Simone:

'I am sure you will not take any notice of him. Mr. Craig sometimes has a warped sense of humour.'

'I wouldn't have brought her here if I hadn't,' Craig said.

The fat man gave Simone a shrug.

'You see what I mean?'

'How are things, Harry?' Craig asked him after the drink question had been fixed up and he'd introduced Harry Kappro to Simone.

Harry told him everything was fine. Then, his face clouding slightly, he said:

'You'd be here strictly on pleasure bent? Nothing in the way of business, I hope?'

'You know me,' Craig told him. 'Pleasure before business every time.'

But Harry didn't appear altogether reassured.

Presently he drifted off and amusedly they watched him putting on the same performance at another table.

Craig and Simone tried to dance, but the floor was impossibly jammed and they gave up. They returned to their table and waited for the floor-show to come on. It was due to start at eleven-thirty. At eleven-thirty-five, Harry Kappro pushed his way round to the dance-band leader and whispered to him.

Five minutes went by.

Ten minutes went by.

Still no floor-show. The dance-band went on playing. Then Harry went over to the band dais and held up his hands.

'Ladies and gentlemen, I am sorry to have to say that Miss Dolores Brant has been taken ill and will not be able to appear to-night.' His audience registered appropriate sympathy and he went on: 'And the rest of the show will begin in a few minutes.'

Craig, telling Simone to wait, hurried after Kappro as he disappeared through a door behind the dance-band. Craig found himself in a narrow passage and ahead of him was a door marked: OFFICE.

The fat man looked up from his desk as Craig closed the door behind him, shutting out the dance music.

'Bad news about Dolores,' he said. 'You made me feel quite anxious about her.'

Harry eyed him speculatively, then he said, slowly:

'Where do you come in on this, Craig?'

'I told you. I'm worried about Dolores.'

'You've got nothing to worry about. Voice gone back on her, that's all. Nothing more to it than that.'

Craig said:

'You mean she just hasn't turned up.'

Harry's face hardened.

'Listen. I like you, Craig. You've helped me. I've helped you. We've never had anything to quarrel about. So why should we start now?'

'Why should we?'

'I'll admit to you, in confidence, of course, that Dolores has not turned up. I have telephoned her half a dozen times, but the number is always engaged. Have a cigar. They're damn good.'

He slid a box across the desk.

'Some other time. Suppose I give her a ring?'

'Why not? You may be lucky.'

But the line was still engaged.

'She's either having a very long chat, or she's left her receiver off.'

Craig went back to Simone. She gave him a questioning look. He said:

'Let's go.'

On their way out, Craig turned and saw

Harry Kappro reappear by the dance orchestra. He was looking across at Craig, his eyes were narrow in his pudgy face. Then the lights went out. A spotlight threw a circle on the dance-floor. The show was about to start.

22

Regent Street and Oxford Street were practically deserted. Presently their taxi rattled down the Bayswater Road and, in a few minutes, drew up outside Tower Court. Craig paid off the driver.

The front door was closed. A faint illumination in the hall showed through the fanlight.

'They go to bed early around here,' Simone said.

Craig lit a cigarette. The flame showed his face taut, his jaw-line grim.

'We'll have to wake 'em up,' he said.

He pressed the bell again.

Came the sound of slow footsteps. Then the lock clicked, bolts slammed back and the door opened. The old man whom Craig had met earlier in the day flicked his gaze over them. Striped pyjamas were visible under his jacket and the bottoms of his trousers. He wore a pair of over-large carpet slippers which slopped when he walked. Apparently he failed to recognise Craig, no doubt because he'd been half asleep before and was only half awake now.

Craig said:

'Miss Brant's expecting us.'

The walrus moustache quivered.

'It is usual to ring the tenant's bell at this time of night. I goes off duty at eleven. At all earlier hours I am available. But not after eleven.'

'We're friends of Miss Brant and we want to go up to her flat. Let's make it snappy.'

'If you ring her bell and she's in, she'll come down. But it's not my job to take you up. Like I said, at all earlier hours — '

'At all earlier hours you are available, but not after eleven,' said Craig. 'I know. But supposing Miss Brant has fallen asleep, or the bell isn't working, or something?'

But the other wasn't to be hustled. He stood there obstinately, and reaching out stuck his thumb on one of several bells.

'If she wants to see you,' he muttered, 'she'll come down. If she's in.'

Craig drew at his cigarette and they waited. The old man stood there, silent, breathing heavily so that his moustache shook like a palm-tree in a squall. Simone smiled sweetly at him. With elaborate casualness, she said:

'Poor Dolores. She always had a weak heart. Suppose she has had an attack to-night. It would be awful if she were left there to die.'

The old caretaker threw her a startled look.

'Er,' he began, 'if you think she — if the lady's ill, I suppose we — that is — er — if you think — '

Simone kept her sweet smile turned on him. She said, diplomatically:

'You are in charge here. I am sure you know what is best to do.'

The other thought for a moment, tugging at his moustache indecisively. Then he braced his shoulders and made up his mind.

'I think perhaps we ought to go and have a look.'

'I think you are absolutely right,' Simone said, and Craig followed her into the hall.

They stepped into the rickety lift. The rope was tugged and they creaked up to the second floor. They got out and the caretaker was fumbling in his pocket for a bunch of keys. He selected one and turned the lock of Number 10.

The flat was dark. Craig explored the wall and found the switch. Across the small hall a door was open. They went in and, as the light in the room came on, the old man gave a startled exclamation.

'Gawdblessmyauntfanny!'

The room was a scene of chaos. A small, round table had been overturned, scattering the contents of a tea-tray. A chair lay on its side, one leg splintered and twisted. Half a dozen gramophone records were in fragments and a radio-gram lay splintered and battered under the window. The telephone had been pushed from its place by a small divan that had been dragged askew.

'Gawdblessmyauntfanny!' mumbled the old man again, through his moustache.

It looked as if Dolores Brant had not only gone in a great hurry, but intended never to return. The room had the appearance of having been stripped of all its owner's possessions. A few novels, magazines and torn-up letters had been left, but any ornaments and pictures had been taken.

Another door opened on to a bedroom and revealed another picture of chaos and hasty departure. The wardrobe cupboard held only bent coat-hangers. The dressing-table drawers were pulled out and empty. Craig crossed to the bathroom. There, too, only an empty bottle of bath salts remained.

'Blimey, if she hasn't done a bunk,' observed the caretaker.

'Tripping over tables and chairs and the radiogram on her way out,' Craig murmured. 'She's gone, all right. But something went on first.'

'You could knock me down with a feather. Cripes! Wot a mess.'

Simone glanced at Craig who was staring round him with a slight scowl.

'This couldn't have been an altogether noiseless operation. Didn't anybody hear anything?'

The old man shook his head.

'It's two floors up.'

'How about the people living on either side?'

'Might have all been out. Usually are in the day-time.' He broke off and said suddenly: 'I wonder if my missis — ? She used to bring up tea for Miss Brant — '

'You mean Miss Brant might have told her she was going away?'

'No,' was the slow reply. Then, with finality: 'No. My wife would have been talking about it. She talks about everythink even when it ain't nothink. She wouldn't have been talking about nothink else all this evening if she'd known Miss Brant was leaving — '

He turned as a figure appeared in the doorway. It was a large woman, swathed in a number of garments topped by a pink kimono with flowers on it. On her head she wore a thing that looked like an oldfashioned bathing cap.

'Osmond,' she demanded belligerently, 'what are you doing up here at this time of night?'

'It's the wife,' the old man said, unnecessarily.

189

Craig stepped forward and said.

'One of your tenants seems to have taken it on the lam.'

The woman gazed round with grim disgust.

'I wouldn't be surprised at anything with that one,' she sniffed. 'Just wait till she gets back. I'll have something to say to her about this. Been throwing another of her parties, by the look of it. Well, I won't stand for it again.'

'I have a hunch she won't come back,' Craig told her, but she didn't seem to hear.

'I suppose she thinks I'm going down on my hands and knees to clear up the mess,' she went on, her voice rising. 'Well, I'm not this time. This is the last straw. I'd like to know what's been going on, though I could make a pretty shrewd guess. I'm not blind, but I'm too respectable to let it pass my lips. Just because she's the artistic type she thinks she can do anything she likes. I'm broadminded, but I know where to draw the line.'

'Save it for a bit,' Craig cut in raspingly,

and the woman was suddenly silent, her mouth open. Craig turned and said to the caretaker: 'She must have decided to clear out some time this afternoon or this evening.'

'She never came down in the lift, that I swear. Not unless — '

'Unless what?' Craig shot at him.

'I went down to the basement for twenty minutes round about four o'clock.'

'Time enough for her to clear out with her luggage.' He turned to the woman: 'You brought up her tea-tray?'

She nodded.

'What time?'

'Ten to three. Near as makes no difference.'

'Was she alone?'

The other shook her head.

'There was a man with her.'

'Know him?'

She shook her head.

'Which puts it between three and four,' Craig mused. 'First one hell of a row, then a sudden decision to clear out.' He snapped at the large woman: 'Would Miss Brant be the sort who'd pack up and go on the spur of the moment?'

She sniffed noisily.

'Oh, she was the sort who'd do anything, regardless.'

Simone, who had been taking a look at the bedroom, suddenly ducked in and then reappeared. She handed Craig a crumpled scrap of paper.

'It had fallen underneath the chest of drawers,' she said.

Craig grinned at her.

'Bright girl.'

He read:

'*Top floor, 24, West Street, Blooms-bury, W.C.1.*'

It was scrawled in pencil. He slipped it into his pocket. To the old man he said:

'Seems that's the way it is. *Cherchez la femme,*' and he grinned again across at Simone. 'How's the accent?'

'Atrocious.'

The woman was beginning to erupt again.

'After all I've done for her. To clear out without a word. I might have known that was the sort she was — '

'This is where we fade,' Craig whispered to Simone, and they left quietly.

In the taxi which they picked up, Craig said, grimly:

'And find the lady it is. She knows something. She was so scared of what she knew, she got out as if all hell let loose were on her tail.'

Simone said:

'Where do you think she has got to?'

He closed his eyes wearily.

'At all earlier hours I'm available, but not after twelve p.m.'

23

Helen drove Jeff to the station, hardly a word passing between them. Since last night she had felt she dare not speak to him. She felt almost afraid of him. Afraid as she might be of a stranger.

At breakfast he had remained silent and morose, his face an expressionless mask.

She tried to smile at him as he got out of the car, but he didn't seem to see her. She saw him hurry on to the platform and then the train drew out. She watched it disappear round the bend, her heart heavy and cold. She turned the car and drove up the hill, along the road under the trees. The big gates had been left open. She drove straight in and parked the car outside the garage.

She went into the sitting-room, where a bright fire was burning. She lit a cigarette and glanced through her diary on the desk and then at a list she had made of things she wanted to get done in the house.

She found it difficult to concentrate. A newspaper thrown on the settee caught her eye. It was the morning paper and Jeff must have thrown it there on his way out. He usually took it with him. She picked it up, casually incurious, and then froze as the headlines stared back at her.

MARBLE ARCH MURDER
GIRL STRANGLED IN MEWS

There was a photograph of the girl and an account of the discovery. It wasn't a very good photograph. The lines were too sharply defined and hard. The eyes too brazen. And the tip-tilted nose didn't look so pertly pretty. It wasn't a good photograph at all, though Helen couldn't know that. She was trembling as her gaze fastened on the account of the murder. Hungrily, yet despairingly, she read it through.

There seemed little doubt that the slayer of Lucy Evans was also responsible for this second dreadful crime. Helen

195

noted the reference to Inspector Marraby taking charge and the report pointing out similar circumstances between both murders.

She sank on to the settee, the crumpled newspaper falling heedlessly from her grasp. It had said the girl must have died around seven o'clock. Jeffrey had caught the seven-thirty-five from Paddington. Paddington, which was only a short taxi-dash from Marble Arch.

The girl had died around seven and Jeff had caught the seven-thirty-five.

That's what she couldn't tear from her mind. That's what she kept on repeating to herself over and over, though she tried to stop it.

He would be taking a drink with a business friend, he'd told her, when he'd 'phoned her yesterday afternoon.

Drink with a business friend.

Girl must have died around seven o'clock.

Seven-thirty-five from Paddington.

Helen stood up with sudden resolution. She couldn't go on like this. She must stop herself thinking like this. She wouldn't think about it. She wouldn't let herself remember that night the girl in Maida Vale had been murdered. She must hang on to her belief that Jeff wasn't lying to her, that his explanations were the truth. She must hang on for dear life. Jeff must be telling the truth. The idea that there was anything else was madness. And her nails digging into her moist palms, she told herself she must, must control her imagination. She mustn't let these stupid little doubts grow like maggots eating into her happiness, destroying her and Jeff.

She stubbed out the cigarette she'd left smoking in the ash-tray with a quick movement. Her face cleared a little and she crossed to the door with a sudden resolution.

She found Mrs. Langley.

'Do you think any of those old keys in the kitchen drawer would fit the door upstairs? The door that is locked?'

The woman shook her head.

'I've already thought of that. I tried them, but they're no good.'

She stared at Helen curiously.

'Never mind. It doesn't matter in the least.'

Helen caught the sound of her own voice and realised why Mrs. Langley was giving her that odd look. Her tone was high-pitched and unnatural. She pulled herself together and tried to speak naturally.

'It's nothing, Mrs. Langley. I'm sorry I bothered you.'

Mrs. Langley watched her go out into the garden and then, with a shrug, turned away and went back to the kitchen.

The sun had come out to make patches of yellow among the dark shadows under the trees. Greyish-white clouds swung lazily across the sky. Soon the sun would be hidden again. A light breeze rustled the leaves and moved through the long grass at the edge of the drive. Something over in the direction of the disused quarry startled the rooks. They circled, cawing raucously, over the woods, swept down towards the river, circled again and then returned, their chatter dying as they settled down once more. The sunshine was dim and then, when the clouds had passed, it glowed again and once more the yellow patches appeared under the trees. Gradually the sun crept across the sky until it was overhead. High noon.

Helen could only toy with lunch. Afterwards she went out and presently found herself at the top of a hill. In the valley the single-track railway line stretched into the distance. A toy train chuffed along slowly. The hills undulated into the haze beyond, black here and there with patches of thick woods.

It was three o'clock when Helen came back to the house. Her mouth was a firm line. In her eyes was a look of determination.

'Mrs. Langley,' she said, and now her voice was without a tremor. 'Ask your husband to take the lock off that door. Come and tell me when it's done.'

In the sitting-room she tried to read a magazine. She smoked a cigarette. She listened to the ticking of the old clock in the corner. She put down the magazine with a restless movement and tidied it up with a number of others glossily askew beside the settee. She wandered round the room. There was nothing to do but wait. The old clock ticked away. Five minutes, ten minutes.

'It's done, madam.'

Mrs. Langley's voice made her jump like a startled rabbit. Helen pulled herself together and went out into the hall. She hurried up the stairs without looking back. She heard Mrs. Langley muttering to her husband somewhere and his mumbled rejoinder. Now the stairs were narrower and darker, creaking in the quietness of the house. The top landing. Helen paused and glanced down through the banisters to the hall below. Mrs. Langley appeared and stood there, looking up. Then she moved away, passing out of view. Helen began to wish she had asked her to accompany her.

The door of the room stood slightly open. A white patch on the paint showed where the lock had been removed. Helen moved slowly towards the door and pushed it open. She could hear her heart hammering.

The room was dim. The solitary window faced north and outside the branches of a tree masked what little light there was. The dull wallpaper made the place look even darker. It was full of furniture, haphazardly stacked. Two bedsteads like iron skeletons, a marble-topped washstand, two tables on top of each other, an old-fashioned chest-of-drawers, chairs and boxes, and the musty atmosphere all added to the room's forlornness. It was as if the room had not breathed for years.

She wondered why it had been so carefully locked. She crossed to the window and opened it. She looked down at the gardener's hut and, just visible towards the end of the house, the edge of the lawn. She left the window open.

She turned to a picture on the wall, which she had not noticed as she came in. It had been hidden by the door. It was a photograph of a group of schoolboys. They were dressed in shorts and jerseys. The boy in the middle of the front row was holding a silver cup. It was Jeff. The face was chubbier, but it was undoubtedly Jeff. He stared back at her, smiling self-consciously. Her face softened tenderly.

She crossed to the chest-of-drawers and tentatively tried the top drawer. It slid open, revealing a heap of old letters, pamphlets and circulars. Most of the letters were addressed to Mrs. Broadhurst. There were two or three slim books in a corner of the drawer. She flipped one open. A name was inscribed inside the cover. Jeffrey Broadhurst.

The next drawer contained photographs. Framed, some unframed but mounted, and small snapshots. Jeff was in many of the pictures.

Jeff in white flannels, resolutely clutching a tennis racket.

Jeff at the wheel of a low-slung sports car.

Jeff in a family group between a man and woman, beaming at the camera.

Helen stared hard at the woman. She felt sure she was his mother. The man had the same jaw-line as Jeff, the same level eyes, though a heavy moustache gave him a severe and uncompromising expression.

The other drawers were full of all sorts of odds and ends. Fancy-dress clothes, false beards, comic hats. The sort of collection people might have used for amateur theatricals and parties. There were a few old gramophone records.

Helen went back to the top drawer again and rummaged through the papers. She took out a passport. Inside was a photograph of Jeff, looking ghastly, his eyes glassy, his mouth turned down at the corners. Involuntarily, she started to smile at it. Poor Jeff. And then she saw it wasn't his name written there. The name was Jeffrey Broadhurst. But it was Jeff's photograph all right. She knew quite definitely what it meant. It meant that the man she had known and loved wasn't really Jeffrey Brook. The man she had married wasn't really Jeffrey Brook. He was Jeffrey Broadhurst.

Suddenly she tensed. Every nerve quivered warningly.

There was a car outside in the drive. She raced out of the room, along the landing and into a room overlooking the front of the house. She pressed against the window and looked down.

The car had drawn up at the front door. It was the local taxi which plied outside the railway station. She saw Jeffrey get out and pay the driver. She saw him hurry up the steps.

She realised she was still gripping the passport. As she moved towards the door she heard Jeff's voice downstairs.

24

There wasn't time to return the passport to the unlocked room. Helen shot downstairs as quickly and as quietly as she could, praying Jeffrey wouldn't hear her. In the bedroom she glanced round quickly for a safe hiding-place. There seemed to be nowhere and in increasing panic she hurriedly pushed the passport into her dressing-table drawer and covered it with handkerchiefs. She looked at herself in the mirror and was astonished to see how calm and normal she appeared. She applied a touch of colour to her face and, calming her jangled nerves, went downstairs.

'Jeff!'

He turned quickly as she came in. She made herself look surprised and pleased, searching his face as she came towards him. His manner was nervous and worried, though he tried to cover it. He took her hand, drawing her towards him with a show of self-conscious tenderness.

'I got back early, darling. Not much going on in town.'

'Pleasant surprise,' she smiled. 'Tea will be in soon.'

Jeff nodded abstractedly.

'Mrs. Langley knows I'm back.' He was obviously trying to be natural and casual as he went on: 'Has a telephone call come through for me?'

Helen shook her head.

'I don't think so, darling. I'll ask Mrs. Langley. Would it be anyone important?'

'It doesn't matter,' he told her hastily. 'It's nothing, really.'

'It might have come while I was out for a walk,' she said. 'Langley or his wife would know.'

'I tell you it doesn't matter — ' His voice rose and he broke off.

'All right,' she said calmly. 'I just thought — '

'I'm sorry,' he muttered. 'I didn't mean to snap at you, Helen. The fact is I — I've got a splitting headache.'

She moved towards him sympathetically, then stopped as she caught the sound of footsteps in the hall. She thought it must be Mrs. Langley bringing in the tea. But the footsteps continued and she heard the front door open and Langley's voice. Someone must have called. Sometimes from the sitting-room the doorbell couldn't be heard ringing in the kitchen.

Jeffrey threw her a quick look and moved towards the door.

'I — I think I know who it is,' he said hurriedly. 'I'll go and see.'

The door closed behind him and Helen waited. Who could the caller be? It became apparent that whoever it was, Jeffrey wasn't going to bring them in. He had been gone two or three minutes, and then Helen crossed and looked into the hall. Quickly she drew back, closing the door quietly. The caller was just going. She hadn't been able to see who it was. Only Jeff's back as he said something which she couldn't catch. She heard the front door close and then Jeff's footsteps across the hall. But he didn't come back to the sitting-room. He went upstairs.

A sudden panic overcame her.

Had he gone to their bedroom? Supposing she hadn't properly closed the drawer and something made him open it? Supposing he found the passport? He would know she had unlocked the room. Or he might even be going up to the top floor for some reason and find the door open and the lock removed. He might bump into Langley and learn what had happened. She bit her lip as she realised she ought to have hinted discreetly to Mrs. Langley that the removal of the lock wasn't to be mentioned to anyone else.

Helen went out into the hall. She started to go up the stairs, then hesitated and drew back. She must pull herself together. She must do nothing that might arouse his suspicions.

She went back to the sitting-room. As she was about to cross to the fire-place, she realised someone was standing by the window and she turned with a gasp.

It was the woman in grey.

The woman who had escaped from the mental home. She had come in by the french-windows, which now stood slightly open. The woman regarded her silently while Helen tried to think what would be the best thing for her to do. Then the woman in grey spoke. Her voice was almost a whisper.

'Shut the door, please.'

Helen obeyed mechanically, mesmerised, as the other came towards her. There was something about her which Helen thought seemed vaguely familiar. She spoke again, her voice still quiet like a whisper.

'So you are Helen. I wondered what you would look like. I have seen you before, but not close to, like this. Oh, you didn't know I saw you. I couldn't let you know I saw you. That would have been a mistake.'

Helen took a step backwards.

'Don't be afraid. There's nothing to be afraid of. Please believe that, my dear. I only wanted to see you before they took me away.'

The whisper cracked into a low sob. Her eyes were no longer fixed mesmerically on Helen's.

'They think I am mad,' she went on, still in that quiet monotone. 'I keep telling them I'm as sane as anyone else. I keep telling them, but they do nothing. They just smile at me and do nothing. And I have to stay there while the years go on and on. Even Jeffrey is against me. Even my son thinks I am mad.'

'Your son,' Helen breathed incredulously, but the other didn't hear her.

'They'll catch me in the end and take me back. I may never get out again. I want to tell you something. You are his wife now and so I must tell you this. Jeffrey is kind and gentle as well as a clever boy. But he needs looking after. He needs understanding. Sometimes he gets nervy and tired. And that makes him difficult. But you mustn't mind that, my dear. Try and understand him. Try and understand him. Whatever he does, put your trust in him always. Jeffrey needs someone like you. It was me he used to need. It's me he still needs, but they won't let me help him. I keep telling them, but they won't let me help him. They keep me away from him.'

She broke off and listened. Then she turned quickly and glided out the way she had come. Helen crossed to the windows after her in time to see the woman in grey disappear among the trees.

Helen's thoughts went round dizzily. It was incredible. Jeff's mother. That poor woman whom the doctors were looking for was Jeff's mother. It was true, all right. She realised, of course, why there had been something familiar about the woman in grey as she stood there. It was that photograph of the family group upstairs. And the likeness between her and Jeff was there, even if it weren't strong. Her mind in a turmoil, Helen was about to go into the hall.

Then Jeff came in.

He closed the door carefully and moved towards her. His face was grim and expressionless. His mouth was set in a hard line. His eyes never left her face. He came towards her slowly. Slowly. Then he paused.

Helen saw he was holding the passport.

'I wanted a handkerchief. I went to the wrong drawer by mistake.'

In the breathless silence that followed it seemed ages before either of them moved. She wanted to go to him, to say something to break that awful nightmare quality that seemed to hang over the room. And then he moved towards her again. He threw the passport on to the table among the magazines. Its pages fluttered noisily as it fell open and then slid to the floor with a thud. Desperately Helen tried to speak. Jeff's hand circled her neck. She tried to scream out, but nothing happened.

Jeff drew her to him and kissed her. She realised he was smoothing her hair. She realised his arms were about her. He kissed her again, eagerly, and then she heard a strange sound. Jeff was crying. It was a choking cry as if the emotion that prompted it was too deep for any words. His sobbing grew quiet. And then:

'Helen. I want to tell you. I must tell you now. I've been such a b — y fool.'

25

The walrus moustache disentangled itself from the blackened pipe and the old caretaker eyed Craig suspiciously.

'Good morning,' Craig said amiably.

'All depends,' the other grunted cautiously. 'Wot trouble you going to start this time?'

Craig gave him a disarming grin.

'Any news of the missing La Brant?'

'Not a sossidge. Good riddance to bad rubbish, I says.'

'And your wife. What does she say?'

'Ditto.'

The pipe pushed its way through the undergrowth of the moustache again and the old man's jaw clamped on it with finality.

'I wondered if maybe she'd sent you any forwarding address?'

The other shook his head, turned and disappeared into his cubby-hole. Pulling a newspaper towards him, he hunched himself busily over the sports page. Craig watched him with amused speculation. He was reminded of a somewhat bedraggled snail tucking itself into its shell.

Deciding there was nothing more he could dig up there, he shoved off. Round the corner, a few yards along, he spotted his next objective. A cabman's shelter and five taxis drawn up before it. He pushed his nose round the door and interrupted a group of drivers in the middle of their mid-morning refreshment. He was rewarded with a concerted gaze of blank disinterest.

'I'm trying to trace someone,' Craig said, his tone duly apologetic, 'who I believe hired one of your taxis yesterday afternoon. About four o'clock, it would be.'

The nearest man, his expression becoming definitely hostile, said:

'So wot, chum?'

'So I think you can help me, chum. Would any of you have been here around that time yesterday?'

The taxi-driver chewed a mouthful of

sandwich reflectively. He swilled it down with a gulp of tea. He gazed round at his companions.

'Four o'clock?' he muttered. 'See, there was me and Fred and Pinky and you, Bert — the four of us — here, if I remember rightly.'

' 'S'right,' one nodded. 'Come to think,' he went on, 'there was a call about four o'clock.'

' 'S'right,' the sandwich-chewer agreed. 'Wot one of us went? You, Pinky, wasn't it?'

The taxi-man addressed as Pinky grunted assent. 'Lady at Tower Court. Hell of a lot of luggage, too. Very near broke me ruddy back, it did. And she only gave me what was on the meter,' he concluded bitterly.

Craig threw him a sympathetic smile.

'She happened to be in a bit of a rush, I'm afraid,' and he dipped into his pocket. 'Perhaps you'd let me put it right.' The five shillings changed hands and Craig asked: 'Could you remember where you took her?'

The atmosphere in the shelter had

thawed simultaneously with the chink of silver.

'Waterloo Station. As you say, sir, she was in a hurry. Had to catch the four-twenty,' she said.

'Four-twenty where?'

Pinky shook his head. 'Couldn't say.'

'Notice any labels on her luggage?'

Pinky frowned and scratched his chin.

'She may have. And then again she mayn't have.'

Craig eased himself from the doorpost. 'Four-twenty from Waterloo

' 'S'right.'

'Which of you gentlemen is prepared to take me there now?'

Pinky was the first to make up his mind.

'Okay.'

Arrived at Waterloo Station, Craig learned that the four-twenty was a stopping train to Woking and points south. He made his way to the appropriate ticket-window, first class. He hoped Dolores Brant would be the first-class type. It might make his job somewhat easier.

'You want to know if a young woman bought a ticket yesterday about a quarter-past four for somewhere on the Woking line?' the clerk queried him dubiously through steel-rimmed spectacles.

Craig nodded. He knew it was a pretty slim chance, but he couldn't think up any other way of picking up the trail. He said:

'She was a brunette. Tallish. Curve appeal.'

The ticket-collector felt with his tongue for a tooth that needed a filling.

'I get the idea,' he said. He shook his head discouragingly. 'I would hazard a guess I sold three hundred and fifty tickets here yesterday afternoon.'

'But they didn't all go by the four-twenty,' Craig reminded him. 'Plus which, they didn't all look like this dish.'

The man pushed his spectacles on to his forehead and rubbed his eyes wearily.

'Can't say I remember her,' he said. 'Sure she went first class?'

'I'd bet on it.'

'I'll see if she made an impression on one of my colleagues.'

He vanished from the window, to return a minute or two later.

'Don't want to raise your hopes,' he said doubtfully, 'but one of my pals says he remembers issuing a ticket at the time mentioned to a dark young woman for Wittons End. Just past Woking. It may or may not be the one you're looking for.'

'He says she was dark and easy to look at?'

'That's it. He remembered her dark eyes and creamy skin, or something. Smartly dressed and all the rest of it.'

It could be Dolores Brant.

'Wittons End?' Craig queried, thanking him. 'Sounds like quite a small place.'

'Sort of a village.'

Craig felt stertorous breathing on the back of his neck and turned to meet the belligerent stare of a red-faced character who looked as if he had a train to catch. Craig patted him on the shoulder and told him magnanimously:

'Your turn now.'

In the taxi back to his office he glanced at an early edition. Front-page stuff about Rita Spear.

'Last night detectives, under Detective-Inspector Marraby, made preliminary investigations by torchlight round the scene of the crime.

'After the body had been removed, police officers were left on guard until first light this morning. At dawn other detectives arrived and made a careful search of the mews.

'Police officers had already visited all-night cafés and coffee stalls round Marble Arch and in the Edgware Road, checking up on the movements of customers.

'Preliminary investigations suggest that the crime was motiveless, as Miss Spear had not been robbed. Money had not been taken from her handbag and a ring was still on her finger . . . '

There was a column of it, with a diagram of the mews and the surrounding neighbourhood. X marking the spot. All the works to keep millions glued to the page with palpitating fascination. It didn't tell him anything he didn't already know.

The murderer couldn't have fixed a better time and place for the job. He had the mews all to himself. Not a soul had come forward to say they'd heard or seen a thing.

Craig dragged at his cigarette. He began to think about Rita Spear the way she had looked opposite him at the little corner table. The tip-tilted nose, the way her hair fell over one eye as she laughed at him.

He remembered the way she'd looked last night, staring up at him from the mortuary slab.

He exhaled slowly, his eyes flinty and narrowed.

He began to think about Dolores Brant and Wittons End. It looked like he'd been lucky over that and it was she who'd taken that ticket all right. Anyhow, he figured he'd soon be able to tie it up for certain. One way or the other.

Leaning back in his chair in the office, he told Simone:

'My money's on her lying low at this Wittons End.'

'Wittons End? I know of it. It is a little place in Kent or Sussex, or somewhere.'

'I'll settle for Surrey,' he grinned at her.

He thought for a moment. Then he came to a decision. He said:

'The way to play it is this way. You drift down to this place. Find out where she's hanging out. Village pub, or something, it could be. You turn on the old Parisian charm and get her talking. You know, win her confidence, and with any luck you may have her spilling why she blew town the way she did.'

'This place sounds so small, I could easily find out where she is staying,' Simone agreed. 'If I once get talking to her, I might convince her we are on her side.'

'Sister-to-sister stuff.'

'That is what I mean.'

'Seems an idea. You'd better get on down this afternoon.'

Craig flipped through the ABC Railway Guide.

'WITTERING EAST & WEST . . . WITTERSHAM ROAD . . .

'WITTON . . . WITTON-LE-WEAR . . . WITTONS END.

'WITTONS END (Surrey).

221

'Miles, 38.

'Map, Sq. 23.

'Pop., 2,701.

'Clos. Day, Wed.

'From Waterloo, via Woking.'

'There's a pub all right. The Harvest Moon.'

Craig found a train at two-eighteen.

'I'll catch that,' Simone said.

She hurried off with a suitcase after lunch. She told Craig she'd 'phone him through that evening. If he were out she'd keep on ringing at intervals until he was in.

After she'd gone a notion which had been growing in the back of Craig's mind blossomed so that he snapped his fingers with sudden decision.

A little while later found him walking into the *Globe* offices. He took a lift to the files department. It was tucked away on the top floor. A plump young woman was in charge and, despite the somewhat vacant look in her pale blue eyes, she was practically omniscient so far as the events of the last ten years went. Craig was just her cup of tea, and it took her no time at all to bang down before him the particular back number of the *Globe* he was interested in. It was ten months back and it carried a report of a fire behind Oxford Street.

'In the early hours of this morning residents of Shilling Street, W.1., were awakened by the crackling of a burning warehouse. The premises of the Soho Silk Company were ablaze. The fire brigade found flames pouring out of the first floor windows and the fire had gained a firm hold of the building.'

The report went on about how the fire-fighters failed to save the building, and concluded to the effect that large consignments of material insured for thousands of pounds had been completely destroyed.

Craig wrote down the name on a slip of paper.

The Soho Silk Company, Shilling Street, W.1.

Meanwhile the plump girl had turned

up earlier newspapers carrying stories of fires which had occurred over a year previously. Another fifteen months before. Craig scribbled their names under that of the Shilling Street firm.

An hour later his list had grown to seven names. They represented fires in the Metropolitan area for the last two years. Craig skipped the places he already knew about.

Craig went out of the *Globe* building and found a 'phone-box on the other side of Fleet Street. Bill Holt's voice came over the wire.

'I'm dropping in on you in a few minutes,' Craig told him.

'That'll be nice. What's cooking?'

'I'll save it till I see you.'

Craig grabbed a taxi and a few minutes later found him in Holt's office. Holt greeted him exuberantly, if somewhat bawdily, and Craig draped himself on the corner of his desk. He interrupted the other's lewd badinage.

'Bill,' he said, 'life is complicated enough without you working so hard at being funny.'

'So I'm not appreciated,' Holt grumbled. 'So all right, Nat. What's the worry?'

Craig slapped down the list he had scribbled out in the *Globe* files department.

'Soho Silk Company, Shilling Street, W.1.

'Angel & Shepley, Ltd., Vauxhall Avenue, Victoria.

'Arctic Furs, Ltd., Exchange Street, E.C.4.

'European Technical Publications, High Holborn, W.C.1.

'Miller, Hamilton & Levinski, Silver Square, Hackney, E.

'Progress Fabric Company, Norman Street, Aldgate.'

Holt looked up from the slip of paper questioningly.

'You remember checking for me the names of firms holding fire policies whose premises had been burnt out during the last six months?' The other nodded. Craig went on: 'The factory at Shoreditch, the Elephant & Castle blaze, the hotel at

Richmond. I was wondering if you'd be nice and do the same for me with this little lot.'

'When?'

Craig grinned at him.

'Thanks, Bill. The sooner the quicker.'

Holt nodded.

'For you, Nat, it shall be sooner than that.' He went on casually: 'What have you got your teeth into this time? Fire-bugs? Or aren't you saying?'

Craig eyed him carefully. 'I'd rather hold it until I'm sure for certain, Bill. Right at this moment you could say I'm just monkeying around with a hunch.'

'Okay, Nat.'

'Soon as it's in the bag I'll give you the tip,' Craig promised him.

The other said he'd like to know and Craig went.

In the street, keeping an eye out for a taxi, he carefully folded the list he'd shown Holt and slipped it into an inside pocket. His fingers encountered another piece of paper. With a slight frown he drew it out. It was the piece Simone had found in Dolores Brant's flat bearing the address: Top Flat, 24, West Street, Bloomsbury, W.C.1.

It reminded Craig he had promised himself a little snoop round there, just in case. He knew it wasn't a very hopeful lead, but he couldn't afford to pass up anything. He got a taxi and told the driver the address.

26

West Street was behind the British Museum.

It was a quiet, old-fashioned street with the typical Victorian frontages of the neighbourhood. Railings ran along the basement area of number twenty-four and there were two or three steps up to a wide front door. The house had obviously been converted into flats, one for each of the four floors.

Craig was slightly surprised to find the door open, but he decided there was a caretaker down in the basement who closed up the place at night.

The hallway was dim, with a damp, musty smell. No one put in an appearance to ask Craig what he wanted. He reached the stairway and began to go up. Each tread creaked loudly, but still no one seemed to hear him.

Suddenly Craig caught another sound. Someone was coming downstairs. Craig paused and listened.

The treads above stopped creaking, too.

There was an unnatural silence over the dim staircase. Craig gave it several seconds and then took two steps upwards. He became certain that the other footsteps were retreating, going back up the stairs. He paused again and listened.

The other footsteps stopped.

It was uncanny. Almost as if that other sound were an echo. Craig went on up again. He knew for certain that someone had been coming downstairs and now they were going back. The someone was going back carefully, stealthily, the stairs creaking however quietly the unknown trod on the old woodwork.

Craig gained the first floor.

The retreating footsteps seemed to be about one floor ahead of him.

He walked quickly along the landing to the next flight. With his foot on the first stair he looked upwards into the dark shadows. There was no sound. The heavy silence hung again over the house.

Craig began to climb. Almost simultaneously he caught the faint creaking of the footsteps, still retreating. Furtively they kept away from him as he went up until he found himself on the second floor.

His foot was on the first stair of the next flight when suddenly he dashed up two stairs at a time. Instantly the other footsteps followed suit, and as Craig made the third floor he heard a door slam above.

Craig grinned to himself. It looked as if he'd scared the other right back to where he'd come from.

There remained one more flight ahead of him, and he presumed the slammed door belonged to the top floor.

Craig went on up into the gloom. The staircase ended in a door. He tried the handle. The door was locked. Whoever had returned to the flat obviously possessed a key. Why had they been so scared of being seen?

Craig stood listening and the silence lapped against him. He was making up his mind whether it would be too tricky for him to risk attempting to break in or whether it would be wiser to retrace his steps. Suddenly he caught a noise inside the flat. A window was being opened. A window that protested noisily. Craig caught it in a flash. The unknown character was making a getaway by the fire escape. Craig dived downwards, taking the stairs two at a time.

A few houses along the street he spotted a narrow opening. It led into an alley on to which the small back yards of that side of West Street opened. He drew back as a figure suddenly appeared along the alley and hurried towards him. He squeezed behind some builders' planks and ladders stacked against the wall and waited. The man went quickly past him and reached the street. Craig could only catch a glimpse of him before he turned out of sight.

He'd have staked all he had it was Anthony Webber of the South London Property Development Company.

27

Craig found himself in the back yard of number twenty-four. A cat leapt from a dust-bin, knocking the lid off with a clatter, and disappeared over the wall. A door at the bottom of some steps led to the basement of the house. At the side a fire escape spiralled upwards.

No one seemed to notice him as he went up quickly and silently past the windows of the first floor, second floor and third floor. The window of the top flat was closed. He peered in and listened. Nobody challenged him. The flat was empty. Gently he pushed the window. It creaked as it had done before. He edged it wide enough for him to duck into the room.

It was fair-sized, drably furnished with grubby-looking curtains and wallpaper. There was a horse-hair sofa, a table, some chairs and a bookcase with a radio on it. Magazines and newspapers were scattered about, and a sewing-basket on top of which were some socks in need of darning. He spotted the note on the table propped against a couple of pipes in an ash-tray.

Called, but you were out. Will phone later. — T.

T.?

Tony Webber, who had dropped that slip of paper in Dolores Brant's flat and forgotten it? It had got brushed aside until smart girl Simone spotted it.

The room opened on to a short passage. Opposite was the bedroom. It was clear the flat was occupied by a man and a woman. Along the passage was a bathroom and a small kitchen.

He went back into the living-room. On a narrow table in the corner was a writing-case jammed full. He opened it. One or two tradesmen's accounts addressed to Vincent, letters to Alfred Vincent and Mrs. Vincent. A well-thumbed notebook caught his eye. It looked as if it were used for keeping accounts. The total at the bottom of the last page of entries — Craig had opened it at random — was £8,320. Pretty big accounts, Craig decided. He tensed suddenly.

Someone was turning a key in the front door.

Voices. A woman's and a man's. The Vincents returning. Craig knew he hadn't a ghost of a chance of getting out of the window without being discovered. The only possible hope was the bedroom. He moved swiftly across the passage just before the front door swung wide. Craig slipped behind the bedroom door. Only just in time. The man and the woman came along the passage and went into the living-room. Craig could see them through the crack in the door. The man looked to be fortyish, with thin hair and a sagging, greyed face. The woman was younger, with over-blonde hair. Her voice was sharp and aggressive.

'There's a note,' Craig heard her say. 'From Tony.'

'What is it?' The other's voice was curiously resonant. He might have been an actor.

'He's been and gone, but he'll phone.'

Craig wondered how long it would be before one of them came into the bedroom. He tried to think up an explanation that could possibly account for his being around. He couldn't think of a thing that made sense, whatever sales talk he gave it.

'What about some tea, dear?' the man was saying. 'I could use a cup of tea very nicely.'

The woman went off into the kitchen and filled the kettle. She came back into the sitting-room.

'The blasted gas has gone again,' she grumbled. 'Got a shilling?'

There was a pause, and then the man said:

'No.'

'We're always putting shillings in the wretched thing,' the woman went on. 'Why can't we get a new stove — or better still, why can't we move out of this dump altogether?' It was obviously a familiar moan. 'I want a place where the kitchen's bang up-to-date. Where you could have service if you wanted it, or there's a restaurant right on the spot.'

'I told you before, Edna, we've got to stick it out a bit longer.'

'I don't see any reason. We could easily afford it. I'm sick of suffocating in this rabbit-hutch.'

'I'll slip out and get some change. Don't let's talk about it now, dear.'

But she wasn't going to let him go until she'd gone over it all over again.

'That's what you always say. I don't see why we can't live better than we're doing. We're making big money. Trouble is, you've got a small mind. You'd go on and on like this. And on. You'd never get out of it. We've got enough coming in now to — '

'Will you shut up about it, Edna?'

'But, Alfred, why — that's what I want to know — why can't we — ?'

'I'll tell you.' There was a little pause and then he took a deep breath. 'I've been meaning to tell you. It may as well be now. I'm going to buy a garage somewhere on the main road where there'll be some business.'

'Are you still day-dreaming about getting out of London?'

Her voice was edgy with scorn.

'It's what we need,' he insisted. 'I mean to get away. Somewhere — somewhere where I can feel safe, so long as it's a place that'll provide a good living. I'm not going to take on anything chancy. You needn't think it. I've worked it out I'd have to invest about four thousand. And another four thousand, say, in reserve in case things were sticky for a while. Don't you worry, Edna, I've learnt my lesson. There's nothing so ghastly as poverty. This time I'm going to be sure I'm on to a good thing.'

'I don't fancy being buried alive in some village or small town, thanks very much.'

'But don't you see? I've got to get somewhere where its safe. I can't go on like this. I can't take this racket much longer. Every day of it puts years on me.'

'What about me?'

'It doesn't affect you the same way. I can tell that. I've always got at the back of my mind what it would be like if — if anything went wrong. If I got put away for five years — '

'You worry too much.'

'Perhaps I do. But people have slipped up before. If they stuck me in prison I'd go mad. I've got to make you understand. We must get out of this business before it gets us. That's why I'm saving every penny.'

She was about to say something when the telephone rang. He gave a startled exclamation.

'Who's that?'

'Don't be so jumpy, Alfred. You're so jumpy. I'll answer it.'

'I'll go and get that change.'

The receiver was lifted and she said:

'Wait a minute, Alfred.' Then into the telephone: 'Yes, it's Edna. All right. All right.'

The telephone was replaced.

'Was it Tony?'

'Yes,' she said.

'What did he say?'

She said slowly: 'We're not doing it after all. There's been some hitch. Tony says he'll let us know in a day or two.'

There was a little silence and then the woman went back into the kitchen. She called to the man:

'Go and get that shilling, dear.'

Craig heard the front door open. This was it. As the front door closed he crossed into the sitting-room. He took a chance and pushed the window open quickly. It creaked all right, but the woman didn't seem to hear it and he was out on the fire escape. He pushed the window shut again and went down without stopping to look back. But he seemed to have made it all right. No one called after him. There were no cries of alarm, no sounds of pursuit.

The cat leapt out of the dust-bin again and dashed up the wall as he crossed the yard to the alley. He pulled the back door after him and paused to light a cigarette. He went out of the alley and reached the street.

28

Simone put through a reverse-charge call, and after a few minutes Craig answered:

'I 'phoned you once before,' she said, 'but you were not in.'

'Been busy. What's new from you?'

'She is staying at the Harvest Moon. I saw her before I came out to 'phone.'

'Where are you speaking from?'

'Telephone-box near the railway station. I cannot speak to you from the inn, of course, and I have had to come all this way to find a call-box. Wittons End does not go in for telephone-boxes.'

'You're sure it's Dolores Brant?'

'Certain. Her name was in the book and I saw her a little later. She matches your description all right.'

'She's there under her own name, eh? No reason why she shouldn't be, come to think.'

'I have not found a chance to speak to her yet,' Simone went on, 'but later to-night it may be possible. It is a very small inn and we are the only guests there, so it should not be difficult.'

Craig said after a moment:

'Watch out she doesn't suspect.'

'I know. I am a little worried about that myself. She might wonder what I am doing here. I told the proprietor I had heard there was a house for sale and I was interested in it. I should tell her the same.'

'It'll do,' Craig said; 'but she's a pretty cagey type. You have been warned.'

Simone laughed.

He thought it made a very nice sound in his ear. She said:

'I will take care. I will do all I can to find out all I can. If there is any more to tell I will 'phone you later to-night. Anyway, I expect I will be back by midday to-morrow with all the news.'

'Get back, anyway,' Craig told her. 'The office isn't the same since you're not around.'

Simone hung up and went out of the call-box. A local train rattled clankety-clank through the station behind her and threw her a despairing whistle. Ahead the lights in the village were popping in the dusk.

Simone paused outside the call-box as a farm labourer approached on a bicycle. He called out a good night as he went past. She was slightly taken aback by the unexpectedness of this friendly greeting, and by the time she found her voice to answer he had disappeared into the gloom.

The inn sign creaked above her as she turned into the Harvest Moon. There was a little hatch at the office through which the proprietor's red face appeared to ask her if she'd like a little something before she ate. Simone took a dry sherry and went up the short oak stairway leading to the parlour. Her high heels clattered on the bare, irregular boards. The parlour was a mixture of black oak beams and dark, depressing wallpaper, but a bright aromatic log-fire did something to counteract the somewhat forbidding atmosphere.

Simone lit a cigarette and sipped her drink. She looked up suddenly as the door which she'd left ajar was thrown wide. Dolores Brant stood there for a moment, stared at Simone, then turned and called downstairs. The proprietor answered her and she told him to bring her up a large whisky. She came into the room and sat opposite Simone. She took out a slim, gold case, tapped a cigarette on it and lit it with a lighter that matched the cigarette-case.

The shirt-sleeved landlord waddled into the room with a round tin tray. With a flourish he placed a whisky before Dolores Brant and went out again. The woman's eyes were dark and slumbrous as she gazed at the drink, and then her slim, scarlet-nailed fingers took the glass. It was half-way to her full, curving mouth when she looked across at Simone and said:

'I have an idea you'd like to talk to me. This is as good a place as any to talk. What do you want to know?'

29

Craig was dreaming the 'phone was ringing. He tried to ignore it, thinking it would stop or someone else, he didn't know who, would answer it. But it kept on ringing louder and louder until the noise seemed to be inside his skull. He came out of his sleep slowly and opened one eye at the jangling instrument. He must have fallen asleep in his chair a little while after Simone had come through from Wittons End.

He focused his open eye on his wrist-watch. It was nearly two hours since Simone had 'phoned. The knowledge shocked him into alert wakefulness. God, he must have been tired. The telephone was still ringing. He looked across at it. Probably Simone again with some news. Quite the fast worker, she was. He pushed himself to his feet and took up the receiver.

It was Bill Holt.

'I've checked that list you gave me.'

'What did it add up to?'

'I'll read it over.'

'I didn't know you could.'

The other's guffaw crashed against Craig's eardrum. When he'd quit laughing, Holt said:

'Here goes: The Soho Silk Company held a fire policy in the name of the South London Property Development Company. Ditto Angell & Shepley, Ltd Arctic Furs were in their own name. European Technical Publications in their own name. Miller, Hamilton & Levinski — the South London Property Development Company. Also ditto and likewise the Progress Fabric Company.'

'So that of those properties four were insured by the South London Property Development Company and two were in their own names?'

'That's it, Nat.'

'You've done a nice job, Bill. I'm more than grateful.'

'For you I'd do it again. Don't forget to let me in on the swindle when you've got it all sewn up.'

'I'll do that little thing.'

Craig hung up.

Thoughtfully he gave himself a drink. He lit a cigarette and swirled the whisky round his glass in little circles. It was the Nicholas Rice racket all over again. This time, he was convinced, with Anthony Webber in Nicholas Rice's shoes. Vincent working in with him. In what capacity, exactly, he couldn't quite figure. But the money entries in the notebook at the flat indicated Vincent was drawing pretty useful cuts. Maybe Vincent was doing the job Jepson had done. Maybe he was the character who actually lit the fires. That was the way it looked to Craig. And this tip-off he'd just had from Holt added further weight to his hunch. He began to think about Jeffrey Brook and Lucy Evans and Rita Spear. Where exactly did they dove-tail into it? The one alive, the two strangled to death. He had to admit the only point of contact seemed to be the fact both girls had worked for the South London Property Development Company and Jeffrey Brook was the fire expert for Pyramid Assurance. Plus, too, his tie-up with Lucy Evans and that business about her threatening him on account of something she knew about him.

Craig stopped thinking about it to knock back his drink. He shook his head slowly. That was where it all started to go haywire. Jeffrey Brook. Lucy Evans. Rita Spear. He dragged at his cigarette and began to try to get another angle on them and Anthony Webber's fire-raising racket.

Then he heard a key turning in the front door. He stubbed out his cigarette and waited.

It was Simone.

She wasn't looking too happy. He didn't say anything as she flopped into a chair except to ask her if she could use a drink, and she said she could. He got her a drink, he lit a cigarette for her and in a minute she began talking.

'I do not think I have done so well.'

He grinned at her sympathetically.

'Don't take it to heart,' he told her. 'Relax and tell me the worst.'

She took a gulp from her glass.

'The worst is,' she said, 'that I have lost Dolores Brant. Vanished into thin air.'

'So she ducked out on you?'

She nodded miserably.

'I am so sorry.'

'What happened?'

'It was she who began it. Telling me about herself. It was after I had telephoned you and got back to the Harvest Moon. She must have suspected why I was there from the moment I showed up.'

'I was afraid she might catch on.' He smiled. 'Frankly, I can imagine you would look a little out of place in a village pub.'

'I suppose that is what it was.'

'You said she started talking. What did she say, anyway?'

'She thought I had been sent by Anthony Webber. I did not say yes or no. I let her believe that.'

'Bright girl,' he said, and she gave him a grateful look. She went on:

'She said she had quarrelled with Anthony Webber. She said it was because he had promised to back some show for her with her in a star part. Then he had changed his mind and she was furious. She explained it made her look silly and she believed he could not have acted like that if he were really in love with her. So she told him to go to hell, there was a violent scene between them and she packed up and cleared out. She went to Wittons End because she had spent several week-ends there and she wanted to lie low and scare Anthony Webber. She wanted to hide away and let him worry about her disappearance.'

Craig said reminiscently:

'So that breaking up of the happy home was all on account of he wouldn't pay up the money for her to be a big star. She makes quite an interesting sort of human being. Or maybe sub-human. I wouldn't know.'

'I would imagine she could be very tempestuous,' Simone said.

Craig nodded. He said:

'It was a neat story she spun for you, anyhow. Do you think there was a word of truth in it?'

Simone gave a little shrug.

'I would not know. She put it over convincingly, but then she is the type who could do that.'

'And after that?' Craig asked her. 'How

did the rest of the performance go?'

'It was time for food, and she said she would join me a little later. Half-way through dinner she had not shown up. I went and asked the proprietor if she were all right, and he seemed very surprised. We went up to her room and she had gone. There was a note, with some money for her bill, saying she would be sending an address for her luggage to be forwarded. She had slipped out a back way.'

'Girl seems to have quite a flair for beating it into the blue.'

'There seemed to be nothing I could do by staying, so I managed to catch the last train back to London.'

Craig asked her:

'She said she suspected you were to do with Anthony Webber?'

'Yes.'

'Wonder why she lied about that?' Craig mused.

Simone looked at him questioningly.

'If she really thought you were spying for him, why should she go to the trouble of giving you that story about herself and

Webber? Come to think, it could have been quite a subtle gag. Suppose she deliberately spun you that yarn to find out if you had come from him. If you had, the chances were that you would have been in Webber's confidence, otherwise you wouldn't have been acting for him. And while she was telling her tale she would have watched you like a snake for an indication that you were already aware of what had happened between them. The betting is you betrayed, quite unconsciously, that you didn't know a thing, which tipped off La Brant you were working not for Anthony Webber, but for someone else.'

'And that is why she vanished, you mean?'

'She was probably scared you were working for the police.'

After a moment Simone said:

'What she told me about herself and Webber might have been true.'

'We'll let it stay that way for now. All the same, I wouldn't mind talking to the luscious La Brant with a nice pair of thumb-screws. Maybe she'd sing a different tune.'

The telephone rang.

'I'll take it,' Craig said.

It was a woman's voice. He thought he'd heard it somewhere before, but he couldn't quite place it. Then she told him who she was, and he smiled bleakly into the mouthpiece.

'This is Dolores Brant speaking. That girl you sent to the Harvest Moon wasn't so bright. But there's one thing I thought you might like to know. That story I told her about why I left town is true. Every word. I didn't run away because I was frightened of — anything else, if that's what you thought. I thought you should know that so that you'll leave me alone.'

'Where are you now, Miss Brant?'

No answer.

Then he heard the click of the receiver at the other end. She'd gone. Craig hung up.

30

Craig slept late the next morning. He breakfasted leisurely in his dressing gown and read through the newspapers. There was nothing fresh about Rita Spear. Nothing fresh either on the Maida Vale killing. Both murders had been pushed off the front page, and it was just the usual Scotland Yard Press Bureau hand-out stuff.

Craig ran a bath and shaved carefully, turning over in his mind the various aspects of the set-up. It was still pretty blurred. Only a few details stood out with any clarity. Worrying round hazy bits didn't seem to produce any new slant from which he could examine them. In the end he relaxed and gave up thinking about the entire business. Experience had taught him that it was around this stage that something always broke. Things which had seemed obscure suddenly appeared in a new light and fitted in and made sense.

He took plenty of trouble selecting a shirt and knotted his tie with meticulous care. He lit a cigarette and went into his office, where Simone was waiting with the morning's mail. There wasn't much to it, but dealing with it and handling various routine jobs took him through till lunch. In the early afternoon Simone came into the office, a hint of excitement in her manner.

'Inspector Marraby.'

Craig took his feet off the desk and stood up. He moved round as the Scotland Yard man came in. He grinned at him amiably. Maybe this was the break he'd been expecting.

'This is an expected pleasure.'

Marraby raised a questioning eyebrow.

'Or do you mean unexpected?'

Craig shook his head and gave the other a cigarette. As he lit it for him he said:

'I had a feeling you'd be dropping in some time. Just one of my hunches.'

Marraby lowered himself into a chair and regarded his cigarette-tip carefully. He looked up to ask:

'D'you always play your hunches?'

'Most times.'

'And most times they're right?'

'Most times.'

'That must make life fairly easy for you.'

'Yes and no.' Craig leaned back in his chair. 'I was just thinking,' he went on, 'before you came in. It's tough being just one man hunting around with so many people against you, or not really for you, anyway. And not afraid of being against you, at that. You have the edge of me every time. People can be against you, but they're scared stiff of you, too. That's where an organisation like yours can get its teeth into a thing like this Lucy Evans and Rita Spear business in the way a private operator never can. You can go at it bang from the start. You can spread out your net and shake from it all sorts of things that, when they add up, can give you the right answers. Me, I have to work from the side. Frankly, I don't like murder jobs, I'll admit it. They're too tough. Murder's all right in detective stories, but in real life it's too tough.'

'You don't have to let those two girls worry you.'

'I try not to. I wish they didn't have to go and get themselves bumped off just when I take on this job for the *Globe*.'

'That cheap circulation booster.'

Craig shrugged.

'Maybe I'll resign when you clean up this mess. Can you use a drink? Or would it be too early in the day?'

Marraby told him it was too early in the day. Craig thought about whether it was too early for him and finally decided it was. Marraby contemplated his cigarette again with his typically aggrieved expression. He distributed his weight more comfortably in his chair and then looked at Craig.

'I'm gratified to learn you think I can finish the job without your assistance,' he said.

Craig didn't answer him. He just waited for the other to go on talking. After a moment Marraby obliged.

'All the same,' he said slowly, 'I just wondered if you might have one or two ideas. By the way, I'm expecting a 'phone call. I told them they could get me here. I hope you don't mind.'

Craig said he didn't mind and the conversation dropped. The inspector got it going again. He said:

'Most of you private detectives think you can do a hell of a lot better than we can.'

'I wouldn't agree to that. I've just been telling you.'

Marraby nodded slowly.

'Of course, working unofficially you can sometimes get away with a fast one which we can't. And sometimes, too, I dare say, you pick up a tip or two which mightn't come our way.' He looked at Craig squarely.

Craig grinned at him genially. The build-up stuck out a mile. He said:

'I wouldn't know about that, either. I thought I had something when I dropped in on you the other day. It seemed I wasted your time.'

The inspector's eyes narrowed a little.

'You didn't fool me at all. You dropped in to see me not because you thought you had something, but because you were trying to find out what I knew that you didn't. It didn't fool me a bit.'

'So I was as unsubtle as that.' He leaned forward across the desk. 'What do you want to know?'

'It occurred to me,' the other said thoughtfully, 'I might, without knowing I was doing it, have given you an angle. If I did, and you've been working on it, you might care to tell me about it.'

'You told me something I already knew,' Craig said, 'that Anthony Webber had talked to you a hell of a lot without saying a thing. Nothing more than that.'

Marraby nodded slowly. He said:

'That was something, anyway. All right, now it's your turn to reciprocate.'

The corners of Craig's mouth quirked. He leaned back in his chair and took a drag at his cigarette. He asked:

'What would I be getting out of it?'

'You never know.'

Craig regarded the other for a moment, then leaned forward again, jabbing at him with his cigarette. He said very slowly:

'Remember Nicholas Rice?'

The other grunted assent. 'You did a

nice job on that,' he admitted.

'Think nothing of it. Maybe I'm doing a nice job now. Only this time it ain't Nicholas Rice.'

Inspector Marraby's head came up with a jerk. He frowned.

'What's this got to do with those two girls?'

'I'm not saying it's got anything to do with those two girls. I'm saying someone's running a fire-raising racket on the same lines as Nicholas Rice. A pal of mine in the insurance business has been tipping me off about the places that have gone up in smoke round London lately. Most of these places were insured by one firm. You would never guess who, would you?'

'The South London Property Development Company,' Marraby said.

Craig didn't bat an eyelash, though he couldn't have been more surprised. He said coolly:

'You've got something there. The South London Property Development Company. And Lucy Evans worked there. She was secretary to the general manager, a character named Anthony Webber. And

Rita Spear worked there, too. Switch-board operator. Remember?'

'I remember. Go on talking.'

'I can't tell you what there was between Anthony Webber and Lucy Evans. I don't know. Yet. Maybe she doesn't fit into this at all. Maybe it's a coincidence. I can't tell you where Rita Spear fits into the picture. I don't know. Yet. Maybe that's a coincidence, too. But I would say this Anthony Webber is fooling around with something. And what he's fooling around with is giving him plenty to worry about.'

There was a little silence. Marraby didn't say anything. Craig gave him a little more time, but nothing happened. So he offered, tentatively:

'Could be some lunatic, or someone, pulled that second murder, imitating the first.'

'Could be.'

Craig went on:

'But you don't believe that. I don't believe that.'

Marraby shook his head quickly.

'Medical evidence proves as near as damn it the same pair of hands throttled the life out of both of 'em. There isn't a doubt Rita Spear died because she knew, or the murderer thought she knew, he'd done the first one.'

'So, when you pinch who did the first job, you're in the clear all the way?'

'Uh-huh.'

There was another short silence while Craig considered whether he should give away what he knew about the Vincents. He rejected the idea and decided he would keep that bit of information to himself. He blew a cloud of cigarette-smoke ceilingwards. Nothing more he wanted to add.

'There you are,' he wound up. 'Does that check with anything else you know?'

The Inspector didn't reply for a few moments. He threw a glance at the telephone on Craig's desk as if he were thinking it was time the expected call came through. Then he said:

'Matter of fact it does check. Confidentially, the Assistant Commissioner is quite worked up over this new fire-raising racket. I think one of the directors of some insurance company flapped to him about it. Anyway, he called a meeting a couple of weeks back. We already knew about a bunch of the places that were burnt out being insured by the South London Property Development Company.'

He seemed to be on the point of saying something else, but just at that moment the telephone rang. Craig took it. It was for Marraby. Scotland Yard. Marraby grabbed the receiver from Craig.

'Yes. All right, go right ahead and apply for a warrant. All right. I'll be right back.'

He replaced the receiver and stood up briskly. His expression was less aggrieved, more purposeful. Craig thought he looked almost a little pleased with himself.

'I'll tell you something, Craig,' he gave a nod towards the telephone. 'Just now it seemed to me you were hinting that perhaps this Anthony Webber murdered Lucy Evans because she'd found out too much about him. Perhaps you were hinting he'd strangled the other girl, too, for the same reason. You were tying in the murders and this fire-bug business very neatly. I just want to tell you you've got yourself tangled up. For once your hunch just doesn't get you anywhere.'

Craig was watching him closely. That 'phone-call meant something. Warrant. A warrant for somebody's arrest. Whose? He said:

'What's news?'

Marraby let a little smile of triumph gleam at the back of his eyes.

'I've just told 'em to go ahead and rope in the real murderer. Young chap. Used to be Lucy Evans' lover. When he started dropping her for someone else, Lucy didn't like it a bit. She tried threatening him, so he had to silence her. Then he had to fix the other girl as well because she knew too much.'

'Tell me more,' Craig said.

'This morning I was pretty damn' sure. Now I know for certain he's our man. Hasn't been at his office all day and he's not down at his place in the country. He's vanished. Bloody young fool, he won't get far.'

'The name wouldn't be Jeffrey Brook,

by any chance?' Craig said.

The other nodded as the telephone rang again. Craig lifted the receiver. It was Simone. She spoke very quietly.

'Helen's here,' she said. 'Helen Brook.'

31

Marraby had gone.

As he got rid of him, Craig couldn't help wondering, with some amusement, what the Inspector would have done had he known the wife of the man he was seeking was at that very moment in the next room.

Helen Brook looked terrible. Her make-up was awash where unheeded tears had streamed down her face. She was crouched in a chair clutching a drink Simone had given her.

'I must talk to you, Mr. Craig. I must talk to you. Something dreadful has happened.'

Craig put a cigarette between her trembling lips and lit it for her.

'Try and take it easy,' he told her.

'Thank you,' she breathed. 'You don't know what I've been through these last few hours. You were the only one I could think of who might help me. That's why I landed myself on you like this.'

'Sure I'll help you,' Craig said. 'Only relax. Take a deep breath and relax.'

Simone told her:

'Yes. Try and do as he says. Everything will be all right.'

Helen threw her a grateful smile. She took a deep breath and made an effort to calm herself. She said:

'Thank God you're here. I drove straight from Quarry House hoping you would be. I know you won't think I'm being a fool. If I only knew what was happening. It's the uncertainty that's so ghastly.'

She took a sip from her glass and went on:

'It was just before lunch. Two men called and asked to see Jeff. I told them he was in London and asked them what they wanted. I realised at once they were police. They said they wanted to ask him some questions. Then they said they were from Scotland Yard. I asked them why they hadn't seen Jeff at his office. They said they'd been along there, but he hadn't turned up. He hadn't been at the office at all. I couldn't believe them. They said didn't I know where he was. I told them I didn't know any more than the office could have told them. I asked them what they wanted to see Jeff about. They wouldn't tell me. I was terrified Jeff would come in and they'd take him away. And it's all a mistake. I know it's a horrible mistake,' she suddenly cried. 'He didn't do it! I know he didn't do it!'

'Didn't do what?'

'These murders. These two girls who've been strangled.'

'I thought the cops wouldn't tell you what they wanted to talk to him about.'

'No. But I'm sure that's what they're after him for. Because,' she gulped, 'because — ' She broke off as if she were afraid to say it. Then she went on more calmly: 'Let me tell you what happened before the police went.'

'Yes,' Craig said. 'Tell me that.'

'The telephone rang and I went into the hall to answer it. It was Jeff. I was so thankful to hear his voice. He said he might not come home for several hours. He told me not to worry and he would be all right. Then one of the policemen came into the hall and asked me who it was. Jeff must have heard him because he rang off at once. I said it was my husband and the policeman asked me where he was speaking from. I didn't know. After that they both went away. As soon as they had gone, I got into my car and came straight here. They'll catch him, won't they? What will they do to him?'

Craig took a long drag at his cigarette. He said, gently:

'Pal of mine from Scotland Yard has just left. Frankly, I think his idea is the same as yours. They're going to try and pin the murders on your husband.'

'Oh, my God,' Helen Brook moaned.

'I know,' Craig said. 'But if he's in the clear, he's got nothing to worry about.'

'I swear he's innocent.'

'He hasn't made it any easier for himself by running away. But maybe he has a reason for that.'

'I don't know. He must have.'

'You were going to tell me why you're so sure he didn't bump off those two?' Craig insinuated.

The other stared at him for a moment. Her face was drawn and haggard. Craig thought she looked very different from the girl he'd met that night at the Café Rouge. She looked terrible.

'I'm trying to think where to begin,' she said. 'It's all so complicated.'

'Take it from the beginning,' he told her, 'and give it me as you think of it. I hear a lot of complicated stories. I'm beginning to get used to disentangling 'em.'

She managed a wry shadow of a smile.

'You see, Brook isn't his name at all. It's really Broadhurst. Jeffrey Broadhurst. But he couldn't call himself that because he didn't want people to know — ' She broke off wearily. 'Oh, dear, I'm not beginning it in the right place at all.'

'Don't worry about that,' Simone reassured her. 'Just talk.'

Broadhurst.

The name struck a chord in Craig's memory. Where had he heard the name Broadhurst before? For the moment he couldn't remember. And then the girl was talking again.

'Jeffrey wasn't going to tell me. He thought everything would come out all right. It would have done if it hadn't been for — the murders. You see, his father used to be head of an insurance company. It went smash and old Mr. Broadhurst lost all his money and then he — died. He — he killed himself.'

Broadhurst!

The name came back to Craig with a rush. He had heard it in Gabriel Warwick's office at Pyramid Assurance. Warwick had shown him that letter recommending Jeffrey Brook for a job. The letter had come from that bankrupt insurance company and it had been signed by Stanley Broadhurst.

Helen Brook was saying:

'Just before his father died, he told Jeff that a lot of heavy claims had drained the firm's money and started a panic, and as a result they went bankrupt. It seemed all these big claims were fire claims. Jeff's father said he was sure these fires were not genuine. He was sure, he said, they were the work of a fire-raising gang. That was over a year ago, and ever since then

Jeff has been scheming to find the man who organised these terrible fires and ruined his father.'

Craig threw a look at Simone. She was listening, fascinated. Craig thought it was slightly fascinating himself.

'So Jeff changed his name,' the other went on, 'and finally got a job with the Pyramid Assurance Company. He managed to — well — to forge his father's signature on a letter saying his name was Jeffrey Brook. He didn't want anyone to know he was Jeffrey Broadhurst. He knew that the head of this fire-raising gang would be on the look-out. You see, his idea was that one day this man would start up the same business again and then Jeff might be lucky enough to get the chance of catching him. Some of the firms might be insured through the very company Jeffrey was working for. After months of waiting, he suddenly found out what he was looking for. It was some fire insurance he'd sold to an office in Victoria Street. It happened twice and Jeff became suspicious, so he deliberately made friends with a girl working at this office.'

Craig was ahead of her, but he didn't say anything. He let her go on without interruption.

'It was the girl they found in Maida Vale.'

'Lucy Evans,' Simone said.

Helen Brook nodded.

'But Jeff didn't kill her,' she said. 'I know he didn't. He couldn't do a terrible thing like that. Besides, why should he have done. It was the other man who must have done it. The man who was scared the girl would betray him to Jeff.'

'Did he say who this man was?'

It was Simone who asked the question.

'No.'

'Didn't he mention any name?' Craig said. 'Anthony Webber, for instance?'

'I don't remember any name. I don't think Jeff told me. I wasn't thinking about it then. I was too worried about Jeff. And then, there was his mother as well.'

Craig's eyes widened a little.

'His mother?'

'She had run away from a mental home. She went out of her mind when Jeff's father committed suicide, and ever since then she'd been in this home. It was near Quarry House.'

'Escaped,' you said.

'Yes. She came to Quarry House and the doctor from the home and another man came after her. Then, yesterday, she came to the house and told me who she was.'

'Poor thing,' Simone murmured.

'You mean they haven't caught her yet?' Craig asked.

'I don't know. I don't know whether they've taken her back or not yet.'

Craig nodded thoughtfully. After a moment he said:

'This girl, Lucy Evans. She'd told your husband who was behind this fire-raising racket, but he didn't mention it to you. Is that right?'

'I think she was this man's secretary,' Helen Brook said. 'That's right. Jeff asked her to look through some private letters in the safe in his office. I think that's how she must have found out about him.'

'One little thing,' Craig queried. 'Your husband hasn't been doing too badly for himself lately.'

'You mean,' the other cut in quickly, 'being able to move into Quarry House? All that money? That worried me, too. When he told me his firm had given him a big job, I tried to believe it. I made myself believe it. But of course it wasn't the truth.'

'You know the truth now?'

Helen Brook hesitated.

'I don't know how to tell you this,' she said. Her voice was pitched very low.

'You've been doing all right so far,' Simone told her.

'You've been doing fine,' Craig said.

'You see, Jeff's idea,' Helen Brook said slowly, 'was that he would make the fire-raiser pay back all the money he'd taken from Jeff's father. When he found out who he was, he threatened to expose him. I suppose — I suppose it was blackmail in a kind of way.'

'In a kind of way,' Craig said.

'I know,' the other said. 'It was wrong of Jeff. But it was his way of revenging himself. Prison was too good for him, he said. The only way he could really hurt him was by making him pay in hard cash.

This man paid him five thousand to keep quiet. He promised some more. Oh, I know you'll say Jeff ought to have gone to the police. But you see, there was another reason, too, why he was determined to get money from this man. He planned to buy back everything his father had lost when he was ruined. That's why he bought Quarry House. It had been sold furnished. Jeff managed to buy it back with everything just as it had been. It was where his family used to live in the old days.'

'I can imagine the way he must have felt,' Craig said.

The girl threw him a look of gratitude. She said:

'One night Jeff went to see this girl. It was the night before we were married. You remember?'

'I remember.'

'We were at the Café Rouge — ' She broke off. 'When I think what a fool I was. I was thinking all sorts of stupid things about him. I expect you realised something was wrong, didn't you?'

Craig shook his head.

'It never occurred to me,' he said.

'Jeff went to where this girl lived in Maida Vale. She was dead. He was terrified, of course. He realised at once how dreadful it would be for him if he were involved. He slipped away, hoping nobody had seen him. He was afraid the police would say he had committed the murder. But he didn't. Oh, he didn't.' She turned to Simone, then back to Craig. 'You do believe me, don't you? I've told you the truth, exactly as Jeff told me. You've got to make the police see it wasn't Jeff.'

She began to sob quietly. Simone touched her arm.

'Why not try and rest up a little? You must be all in.'

After Helen Brook, aided by sedatives, had fallen into a sleep of utter exhaustion, Simone came into Craig's office. Her expression was anxious.

'What do we do?' she said.

Craig leaned even further back in his chair.

'All we have to do is find the character who really did strangle the two girls.'

'You think it is going to be as easy as that?'

He looked along his nose at her sardonically.

'I will have my little joke.'

'Who else could it be?'

'How about this Anthony Webber? It could be he's the murderer and also number one fire-bug-in-chief. In person. How d'you like that?'

'I like anything if it proves that Helen's husband did not do it.'

'I take it you were impressed by her story?'

She nodded.

He regarded her silently for a moment. Then, as if reaching a decision, he took his feet off the desk and got his hat. In answer to her inquiry, he said:

'Just a notion I'm working on.'

'You do not want to tell me?'

He shook his head, smiling at her bleakly.

'I don't think I ought to tell you. It's not strictly legal.'

The office door closed behind him.

32

I

'The Fiddler's Dog' was a basement café off Greek Street. Run by a character rejoicing in the name of Barnaldo Rosen, it was open at all hours of the day and night. Barney's clients knew good coffee when they tasted it and, at twopence a cup, Barney's coffee had got what it takes. More than any other coffee for miles around. Added to which, in winter all sorts of queer customers, with no hope in their eyes, and less food in their bellies, could stick around all night in the humid warmth just toying with a twopenny cup.

Every now and then Barney would turn the coffee urn and the sausage-rolls over to his large Italian wife, while he went out into the night to some destination unnamed. Barney's vanishing act always took place at night. A few hours later he would return to 'The Fiddler's Dog' and resume his duties. If an inquisitive police officer should subsequently inquire as to his whereabouts on the previous evening, Barney's alibi would be invincibly corroborated by his wife. Also by Barney's customers.

The observant might notice that such episodes in Barney's life were invariably followed by some display of his prosperity. Such as a new brooch for Mrs. Rosen, or a new tie-pin for Barney himself. Barney had rather a taste, if a somewhat flamboyant taste, in jewellery.

'Wotcher, Mr. Craig,' Barney said. 'I see you're working for the *Globe* these days. How's business?'

'Crime's on the up-and-up, you'll be glad to know,' Craig told him. 'Where's Slate?'

The other gave him an uncompromising stare.

'Why?'

'Slate and I are due for a little friendly conversation. All right with you?'

Craig was aware that Barney's show of hostility was merely technique implying no fundamental reluctance to facilitate business between friends.

'In the back room.' Barney jerked his thumb. 'You can go through.'

Barney's back room was in no sense a hide-out. It was merely a rendezvous where Barney's more intimate companions could play cards and chat of this and that. Barney had taken considerable pains to furnish it quite attractively in a repulsive sort of way. Only one individual was present. He was bent over a newspaper.

'Slate. Pal of yours.'

Slate Kellett had once been pinched on a charge of burgling a house in Kensington when he had, in fact, been chatting to Craig in a Shaftesbury Avenue bar at the time. A fact which Craig had been happy to pass on to the magistrate. Slate lifted his head from his newspaper and a smile made a toothless gap in his face.

'Okay?' Barney asked him.

'Okay,' the other nodded. Barney faded.

Craig didn't waste any time sparring around. He said:

'Listen, Slate. Would you open up a safe for me?'

An expression of child-like innocence spread over Slate's features.

'I don't quite fathom you, Mr. Craig.'

Craig grinned.

'Relax, pal. We're talking turkey.'

The other accepted a cigarette and dragged at it thoughtfully. He let two streams of smoke curl up from his nostrils. He said:

'I don't say as how I wouldn't know how to go about it, provided it was all above board. Where is it?'

'Maybe I should explain. It isn't my safe.'

'Not your safe?'

Craig shook his head.

'Oh.'

The innocent expression was beginning to return to Slate's face

'The safe is in an office, Victoria way,' Craig told him. 'Something inside it I want to get hold of.'

The other nodded sympathetically.

'I know the feeling, Mr. Craig.'

Craig grinned at him slowly. He said:

'It's what you might call evidence. I'm doing a little job for the *Globe*.'

'I know. I reads the *Globe*. I reads all the newspapers. Can't think why. Full of tripe. Nothing personal intended,' he added hastily.

'Don't mind me. So you'll do this little thing for me?'

'If you say so, Mr. Craig. I suppose you might say we would really be working on the side of the law?'

'You might say so. Only don't kid yourself. We could go to the cooler for this. It's got to be a neat job, Slate. And a quick getaway.'

The other spat a bit of tobacco from the side of his mouth.

'When?'

'To-night.'

'Cripes! I must have a look at the place first. Where is it?'

'The South London Property Development Company, Victoria.'

'They got a night-watchman? Or caretaker?'

'I wouldn't know.'

'There you are, Mr. Craig,' Slate told

him. 'You got to know about these places aforehand.' Two more wisps of cigarette-smoke drifted from his nose. 'If it's one of these old dumps it mightn't have a caretaker.'

'This is a pretty old building.'

Slate thought for a minute.

'Tell you wot. I'll go down and look it over, and I'll meet you there. Say seven o'clock. I'll give you my opinion and, if it's okay, I'll do the job there and then. That's all I'll say now. Can't take no chances, Mr. Craig. You can't really. But, as I say, if it's okay, you can trust me.'

Craig told him, all right, he would settle for that.

II

The luminous dial of his wrist-watch said two minutes past seven. Slate should be showing up. The closed, heavy doors presented a pretty tricky problem, he decided, eyeing them from his position across the street. Came a touch on his elbow and Slate was apologising for

283

keeping him waiting.

'Only just finished spotting the flattie,' he said.

Spotting the flattie was the technique of locating the nearest cop and estimating how long would elapse before his beat brought him past the back of the offices.

At this moment, Slate said, the aforementioned cop was a couple of streets away. It was a no-caretaker dump, he said.

They crossed over and turned down the street running alongside the block.

'We've got five minutes,' Slate said.

They stood before a narrow door. Slate gave a glance up and down the street and then there were metallic sounds from the lock. Came a click, and the door swung open. They were inside with the door closed behind them. A pool of light from Slate's torch danced ahead.

'Lead the way.'

Craig led the way to the front of the building to the staircase.

'You don't mind walking?' Slate's tone was one of sarcastic solicitude.

They went up the stairs like two swift

shadows. Outside the offices of the South London Property Development Company the shadows paused. A passing bus made a distant mumble. A taxi honked. But the building was silent.

'Okay,' Slate breathed. Followed more metallic sounds, then a sharp click. Craig pushed the door open.

Slate's torch swept the main office. For a moment it hovered on the switchboard. In that moment Craig was remembering again the piquant face of Rita Spear.

'It's in here,' he said, and Slate followed him to the frosted-glass door. It was unlocked and the torch beam came to rest on the black square in the corner of the room. They crossed to it and Slate muttered:

'Like breaking into a kid's money-box. Only got to breathe on it, I have, and it'll fall apart.'

'So go ahead and breathe,' Craig told him. 'Then let's get out of here.'

Slate bent before the safe. There were the metallic scrapings and probings. Finally a grunt of satisfaction and he gave the handle a turn. The heavy door swung open.

'It's all yours, Mr. C.'

The top shelf was crammed with ledgers. Below, bundles of papers, and a box file. On the bottom shelf cheque-books, note-books and more papers. Craig quickly sifted through the papers, then his interest focused on the box file. He took it out and opened it. Clipped inside was a bundle of old letters.

Slate was humming softly under his breath.

'Some light,' Craig told him.

He turned over the letters. Some handwriting in green ink caught his eye.

'Darling, I am thinking of you always. There is no one else for me but you. Why don't you telephone? Did you get my other letter? I mean what I said, darling. If you don't stand by your promise I shall go to the police and tell them what your game is. I have every right to make you keep your promise to me. You can't get out of it. I've had a look through some letters in your safe and have found out who you're working for. I did it for a friend of

mine. You see, he told me how you really make your money. That's how I know. I mean what I say.

Lucy.'

Craig remembered the beginning of the fragment of the letter he'd found in Lucy Evans' room. He thought it was identical with the beginning of this letter. Lucy had thrown the half-begun letter away, he supposed, and started again. This was the final draft she had written to Anthony Webber.

It was beginning to add up.

Webber had been Lucy's boy-friend. It was he who was going to walk out on her. Lucy's friend who tipped her off about Webber would be Jeffrey Brook. That fitted in. He'd persuaded her to dig through Webber's safe. Armed with the knowledge she'd picked up, Lucy had tried to blackmail Webber into marrying her.

That was how it went, Craig told himself. He glanced at the letter again:

' . . . *I've had a look through some*

*letters in your safe and have found out
who you're working for. I did it for a
friend of mine . . .'*

The letters in the safe?
That meant those he was holding right
now.
Quickly he flipped through them for
the first letter. Suddenly he couldn't see
any more. Suddenly the torch had gone
out. He started to say something to Slate
and then knew someone else was there in
the darkness.
Craig kept very still. His eyes got used
to the gloom and he made out the figure
at the door. The intruder wore an
overcoat and his hat came down over his
eyes. The lower part of his face seemed to
be covered by a scarf.
'I'll take those.'
The voice was either deliberately
disguised or muffled by the scarf. It
reached Craig as a blurred whisper. It
sounded eerie and unreal in the dark
silence. The man moved forward.
'Put the letters on the desk. Drop that
torch and put up your hands.'

Craig saw the glint of something in his hand. The bundle slapped on to the desk simultaneously with Slate's torch hitting the floor. The man grabbed the letters, pushing them into his pocket.

'Get away from the safe.'

They moved aside as the other, jerking his automatic at them, reached the safe and, with his free hand, quickly went through the papers on the shelves. Apparently he didn't find what he wanted. He backed to the desk. He pulled open a drawer and searched it with his free hand. He pulled open all the drawers in turn, still without finding what he was after.

'Did you take a gold watch?'

'No,' Craig told him.

The other stared at him for a moment, then carefully backed towards the door.

'If you try to follow me, it'll be your last move.'

Then he was gone.

'Cripes,' breathed Slate as the outer office door closed, 'we been hijacked!'

'You'd better call the police,' Craig told him sardonically and lit a cigarette.

33

The morning newspapers worried Jeffrey Brook's disappearance to death.

In his taxi on the way to Scotland Yard, Craig read the *Globe's* front-page story. There was a photograph and Jeffrey Brook's description. The photograph didn't do anything to flatter him. There was no revelation of his real identity, nor any hint that he might not be the murderer. Craig had kept his knowledge to himself. He didn't intend the *Globe* should shout it from the housetops until he knew who really had strangled Lucy Evans and Rita Spear.

In Marraby's office, Craig told the Inspector:

'Thought I'd look in to tell you that my hunch isn't working out so badly after all.'

'You mean Anthony Webber?'

'I think you might pull him in. Just for the fun of it.'

Marraby looked at him sharply.

'This bee in your bonnet about Webber still buzzing, eh? When I'm working overtime on this mug Brook. I tell you, Craig, it's an open and closed case. Everything fits. My money's on Brook. Maybe you have got something on Webber. I should worry about him, shouldn't I, right now?'

'You should, too,' Craig said. 'I'll tell you something. Lucy Evans didn't write that letter to Brook. She wrote it to Webber. I can go on talking, if you like.' The Inspector frowned impatiently. 'Webber's in this fire-bug racket, like I said. Not the head boy. But he's in it. Up to the neck.'

'Wait a minute. You say she wrote to Webber. How do you know?'

Craig grinned at him.

'I took a look in his safe and saw the letter she wrote him after she'd thrown away the bit — er — you found.'

'You had a look in his safe. When was this?'

Craig waved a hand casually.

'I happened to be in his office.'

'Where's the letter now?'

'I wouldn't know,' Craig said, wishing like hell he did.

Marraby eyed him suspiciously. His expression grew more aggrieved. He was convinced in his own mind he had found the murderer of Lucy Evans and Rita Spear. At the same time he had to admit Craig's story, coming on top of their conversation of yesterday, might be worth looking into. He realised it was not impossible that there might be some tie-up between this fire-raising racket and the stranglings. He said to Craig:

'You sure about this?'

Craig nodded.

'I'll stick around while you check it. How's that?'

Marraby paced over to the window and stared out for a moment. Then he made up his mind.

'Perhaps a little heart-to-heart with him wouldn't do any harm.'

He picked up the receiver and asked to be put through to the South London Property Development Company.

'We'll ask him if he'd like to pop along,' he told Craig.

It was half an hour later when Anthony Webber was shown in. From his attitude, he might have been paying a social call. He exuded genial charm, though his eyebrows met in a slight frown when he saw Craig.

'Surely we've met before,' he said.

Craig gave him a pleasant smile.

'Take the weight off your feet, Mr. Webber,' the Inspector said. 'I hope you'll forgive us for bothering you. I'm sure you must be an extremely busy man and we're very grateful to you for coming along.'

'Anything I can do to help?'

Marraby went on:

'This is just a formality, you understand?' The other's expression showed he understood. 'We merely wondered if you might be able to offer some further information which might help us over these two murders. Lucy Evans and Rita Spear.'

'Quite so, Inspector. I, myself, cannot help feeling a certain sense of responsibility regarding these two ghastly tragedies. Of course I only knew them as employees and exercised no influence whatsoever

over their private lives. Still — well — '
He broke off and spread his hands, then
pressed them together again. 'If there is
any way I can assist you to apprehend the
dreadful person or persons responsible
for their deaths — '

'Thank you very much, Mr. Webber,'
the Inspector cut in. 'Glad you see it that
way.'

Webber took out a long, gold cigarette-
case and flicked it open, offering it to
Marraby and Craig. The Inspector shook
his head and Craig indicated a cigarette
he was already smoking. The sergeant
Craig had met with Marraby at the house
in Vale Crescent came in unobtrusively,
propped himself casually against the wall
and thumbed a shorthand notebook.

Inspector Marraby coughed and asked:

'Do you remember, Mr. Webber, the
night of Miss Evans' murder?'

Anthony Webber allowed a spiral of
cigarette-smoke to curl up from his
mouth.

'How do you mean, exactly? Remember?'

'Could you give me an idea of your

movements from, say, six o'clock that evening until, say, nine?'

'I'm afraid I still don't quite understand.'

Marraby looked so aggrieved Craig almost expected him to burst into tears.

'Now, Mr. Webber. As I said, this is merely a formality. If you would like to give us some idea where you were between the times I've mentioned on that particular evening, we shan't need to trouble you any further. It's just a routine job for me as well as for you. I think we ought to be able to get through it without any trouble.'

Anthony Webber frowned thoughtfully.

'I find it hard to recall exactly where I was. Between six and nine,' he murmured, half to himself. 'I think I went to my club. Yes, Grey's Club, St. James's.'

'What time was that?'

'I went straight from my office. That evening it was between five and six.'

'What time did you leave the club?'

The other thought a moment, then:

'About an hour later, I think.'

'Where did you go then?'

'I had dinner at Duprez's, Jermyn Street. I was probably there till half past seven.'

'Then?'

'Then I visited a friend of mine.' Very slowly.

'Where?'

'Bayswater.'

'His name, please?'

'Is that absolutely necessary?'

'It would help.'

'It was a woman friend. I should like to keep her name out of this.'

'I'm sorry, but — '

'Very well. Miss Dolores Brant. She lives at Tower Court.'

'How long did you stay with Miss Brant?'

'An hour. Perhaps a little more. So far as I can remember, I arrived there at a quarter to eight.'

'So you left Duprez's at seven-thirty or so, and arrived at Tower Court, Bayswater, at seven forty-five. You took a taxi?'

The other nodded.

'And you remained with your friend — Miss Brant — from a quarter to eight until about nine. Right?'

The other nodded again.

'I went straight back to my club,' he said. 'I think the time was about twenty past nine when I reached Grey's.'

'That seems all very straightforward, Mr. Webber. If we can just check that over. The times.'

Marraby nodded to the sergeant who came forward and referred to his notebook.

'Between five and six to approximately seven at Grey's Club. Seven to seven-thirty at Duprez's restaurant. Seven-forty-five to nine at Tower Court, Bayswater. Nine-twenty arrived back at Grey's Club.'

'Okay, Mr. Webber?' the Inspector queried.

'As near as I can remember.'

Marraby's expression became less morose. He became almost expansive.

'That's fine, then, Mr. Webber. We're very much obliged to you.'

Anthony Webber rose, carefully brushed some tobacco-ash off his suit and smiled blandly. The sergeant held the door open for him and followed him out.

'I still think it was an idea,' Craig told Marraby. 'That alibi could be phoney.'

'Sounded all right to me.'

'I'm not doing a thing this morning,' Craig said. 'I'll run the rule over it for you.'

Inspector Marraby shrugged.

'If you want.'

Craig wasn't deceived by the other's casualness. Marraby was mean about giving his thoughts away and was just as likely to be suspicious of Webber's alibi as not. If he did think there were holes in it, he'd work his men into nervous wrecks trying to break it down. At the door Craig told him:

'One thing. You won't find Dolores Brant at that Bayswater address. She took her flat apart night before last and headed for a rustic life at the Harvest Moon pub, Wittons End. When last heard of, the bird had flown from there, too. Destination unknown.'

'Get around, don't you?' Marraby said.

Craig grinned at him.

'Sometimes you think I'm just a pain in the neck. Sometimes you think I know a thing or two. I'll call you later.'

Marraby stopped him.

'Keep your trap shut about this,' he warned him.

'Trust me.'

'I never trust private dicks.'

'I'll personally see what I can do about restoring your faith.'

34

It was unlikely he'd pick up much information from Grey's Club. Without authority from the police, he knew he wouldn't be able to shake them down if they preferred to be sticky. And they probably would be sticky.

Duprez's, however, was something else again.

The restaurant was submerged in a behind-the-scenes atmosphere. Tables were stacked on top of each other while a couple of cleaners raised the dust off the floor. Craig found a shirt-sleeved waiter checking over a list that might have been the menu for lunch.

'Mr. Duprez's in his office,' he said, waving a hand vaguely towards the back of the restaurant. As he spoke, a bald little man with a waxed black moustache appeared. The waiter called to him. 'Someone for you, Mr. Duprez.'

'M'sieu requires something?'

'The name's Craig. I'm taking care of a little notion I have. I was wondering if you'd like to help me.'

Duprez eyed him narrowly.

'Why you should think I can do something for you?'

'Why you should think I can do something for *you*. Some other time.'

'You are from the police?'

'Yes and no,' Craig told him. 'I'm trying to save you being bothered by the police.'

The other fiddled with his moustache for a moment. Then:

'You will come into my office, perhaps?'

Craig followed him into a small, untidy room. There was a roll-top desk with papers scattered all over it and a large bowl of flowers on a chair. There was no window and the room was very stuffy. Duprez moved the bowl of flowers and Craig parked himself.

'Now we can speak,' Duprez said.

'You have a client name of Webber. Anthony Webber.'

'M'sieu Webber,' he nodded, 'he comes here many times.'

'Would you remember M'sieu Webber dropping in for dinner last Tuesday week? Would you remember that?'

'Last Tuesday week?'

Duprez began to search back in his mind. He gave an exclamation and said:

'That is the time when M'sieu Webber have *sole meunière*, I think. Let me see.' He turned to the desk and ruffled through a bundle of old menus. 'No. It is wrong. On last Tuesday week we have no *sole meunière*. I remember now. The gentleman asked me for sole and I tell him how I regret not to have any on that day. M'sieu Webber enjoy *sole meunière* very much, you understand?'

Craig said he understood.

'*Eh bien*. But this evening we have no sole and instead he has a very nice *entrecôte de veau*. Yes, that is right. It is here, you perceive, on the menu for the evening of last Tuesday week.'

'So now we know that on the night in question, M'sieu Webber was unlucky and had to make do with *entrecôte de veau* instead of *sole meunière*. We're doing fine.'

'I do not know what you wish to ask about the gentleman.'

'What time did he arrive and what time did he beat it?'

'Always M'sieu Webber is arriving at seven.'

'Was that the time he came in on that night?'

'I cannot remember exactly. But it would be about that hour.'

'And left?'

Durez's eyes suddenly glinted.

'But that is simple,' he said quickly. 'The gentleman departed at seven-thirty exactement. I remember him insisting to have the *entrecôte de veau* very quick because he must leave by seven-thirty. *Et alors*, by consequence, he departed at seven-thirty. On the minute. I remember distinctly.'

'He didn't happen to mention why the rush?'

The other shook his head.

'There is no reason why he should discuss it with me. Is it permitted for me to ask why you wish to learn these things?'

'It is permitted for you to ask, but not permitted for me to answer.'

Duprez shrugged and produced his professional smile.

'One must be discreet,' he murmured. 'It is understood.'

'You've got something there,' Craig told him. And, deciding he'd got all he could, he pushed off.

So Anthony Webber had, in fact, left the restaurant at seven-thirty. It could be he had deliberately taken care to impress the time on Duprez. He had certainly made enough of it so it would stick in Duprez's mind. Had it been part of a prepared plan to build up his alibi, or had he really been in such a hurry to see Dolores Brant at her flat. A quarter of an hour had elapsed between Anthony Webber quitting the restaurant and arriving at Tower Court. According to his alibi, he had made the journey by taxi.

Craig, standing outside Duprez's, grabbed a passing taxi and told the driver:

'Tower Court, Bayswater. And the sooner the quicker.'

The time by his watch was exactly ten

minutes to eleven. Would it be possible to do the trip in, say, only ten minutes? he asked himself. The taxi had swung into Piccadilly. Now they were coming out into Park Lane. They reached Marble Arch. His eyes kept returning to his watch. He realised he wasn't going to make it inside the ten minutes. It was already three minutes to eleven. The taxi swung left and exactly four minutes later they were drawing up outside Tower Court.

Eleven minutes.

Allowing for greater speed at night, Craig decided it would be possible to get from Duprez's to Tower Court inside ten minutes, assuming Webber had grabbed a taxi immediately on leaving the restaurant. The route, of course, would have been different from Marble Arch to Vale Crescent. He'd have gone straight up the Edgware Road.

Craig said to the driver:

'Back to Marble Arch and from there step on it to 5, Vale Crescent.'

The driver turned a puzzled look on him, then hunched his shoulders and they headed for Marble Arch. Craig took the time at Marble Arch. Four and a half minutes later they pulled up outside number 5, Vale Crescent.

Four and a half minutes.

Eleven and a half minutes from Duprez's to Vale Crescent. Allowing for better times at night, Craig reckoned Anthony Webber could have made it in nine minutes, which left him six minutes to strangle Lucy Evans, grab another taxi and beat it to Tower Court. Say three minutes for the murder. He told the taxi-driver:

'Know all the short cuts back to Tower Court?'

The cabby regarded him with a certain amount of pity.

'You mean you wanter go back again?'

'That's the gag.'

The other's mouth opened slightly as if to say something, then he hunched his shoulders and they headed for Tower Court. They slewed round corners, cut through side-streets. It was just four minutes later when they pulled up again outside Tower Court.

The driver poked a nose that quivered with contempt through the window.

'Now wot?'

'It's been a nice ride. Now we'll go home,' and Craig gave him the address.

A pent-up sigh and the nose withdrew. Scowling, Craig lit a cigarette.

Allowing for an almost impossible series of perfect circumstances, Anthony Webber could not have got to Vale Crescent from Duprez's, bumped off the girl and made Tower Court in fifteen minutes. If Dolores Brant backed up his alibi that he was at her flat at a quarter to eight, Anthony Webber was in the clear.

If Dolores Brant testified Anthony Webber had been with her at the time he'd specified. That was the thing and somehow Craig had the feeling that when Dolores Brant did turn up she'd corroborate Anthony Webber's story to the hilt.

When he got back to the office, Simone practically fell on him.

'Jeffrey Brook. He left ten minutes ago.'

35

I

'You could knock me down with a feather-weight,' Craig said. 'Where's he gone?'

'We do not know — '

He cut in:

'His wife — she saw him?'

Simone nodded.

'He had found out she was here. That is why he came. He wanted to see her and tell her he was all right. Not to worry.'

'How did she take it?'

'All right. I left her quiet in the sitting-room. She begged him to give himself up to the police. She told him it would only make matters worse for him in the end if he did not. But he said no. He kept on about he was going to get someone first. Helen began to cry — '

'What's this about him going to get someone? Who?'

She shrugged her shoulders.

'He didn't say a name?' Craig persisted.

'No. He did not say any name.'

'So he just looked in to tell Helen not to worry about him, and then he cleared out, threatening he was going to bump somebody off?'

'It sounds silly, I know. But that is what happened.'

Craig picked up the receiver.

'What are you going to do?'

'Pass the word along to Marraby.'

There was a little silence while she looked at him disbelievingly. Then she said quietly:

'You are not going to help them catch Helen's husband?'

'I work with the police,' he told her. 'Not against them.'

Suddenly her eyes flashed.

'But what about Helen? Is she not to be thought of as well as your Inspector Marraby?'

He replaced the receiver, staring at her. 'What is this?'

'It does not matter to me,' she said and

then, deliberately mimicking his tone: 'Think nothing of it. After all, you are a detective,' she went on. 'The feelings of your friends do not count. I understand that. You are someone hired to do a job and you do it. Why should you worry about that poor girl. Besides, Inspector Marraby will be very pleased to receive your information.'

He suddenly caught hold of her and shook her so that her hair fell over her face. Then he tilted her face upwards and looked down at her. Her nose was shiny, her eyes were brimming with tears.

'You're putting on weight,' he said. 'You're getting to be quite a big girl. Why are you acting so kittenish. I don't like hearing you talk this way.'

'I am sorry,' she said.

He realised he was still holding her. He let her go reluctantly.

'I think all this has been getting on my nerves a little. I am sorry.'

'Think nothing of it,' and his grin mocked her.

'It sometimes gets a bit nervy round here. But let me tell you before you start trying to run my business, you should know the best way to get along is to keep your client in the clear with the cops. Right along. That's what I'm doing for Jeffrey Brook — though he isn't even a client at that. Quickest way to help him is to get these murders pinned on whoever did them. Marraby wants to do that very thing and I'm out to help him. Bringing in Jeffrey Brook won't hurt him if he's innocent. If he's trying to play hero and keeping something useful back, it might even get him talking, open up a new slant on the business.' He picked up the receiver again. 'Now, get the hell out of my office. I'm busy.'

Inspector Marraby thanked him for his tip-off. Craig gave him all the story of Helen Brook's arrival and her husband appearing and vanishing again. Marraby remained unconvinced of Jeffrey Brook's innocence.

'It won't be long before he's picked up,' he said. 'If he sticks in London, he'll be caught. If he tries to get out of London, he'll be caught. Both ways he'll be unlucky.'

'What about his threatening to bump someone off?' Craig asked.

The other said:

'Probably he was just steamed up. If he really is going after someone, but we don't know who that someone is, we can't warn them. But don't you worry, we'll rope him in before he has time to do any more damage.'

Craig let it go at that.

After he'd rung off, Simone came into the office. She had tidied up her face. Her mouth was shiny with fresh lipstick. She smiled at him a little shakily. Then she said:

'There is a call waiting for you from Helen's uncle. He is in London. He wanted to speak to her, but I was not sure. I thought you might want to talk to him first.'

Craig nodded.

'I'll take it,' he said.

'I believe Mrs. Jeffrey Brook is staying with you,' the voice said over the wire. 'I'm her uncle. Albert March.'

'What's on your mind, Mr. March?'

'I wonder if I might speak to her?'

'How did you find out she was here?'

'Quite simply,' the other said blandly. 'I telephoned Helen's home and the house-keeper told me where she was. I understood she had instructions only to give the address to her husband or close relatives.'

'Hold on, I'll get her.'

He went into the outer office.

'I'll tell her,' Simone said. 'She can take the call in the sitting-room.'

She came back in a few minutes.

'He's calling here,' she told Craig. 'He wants to see Helen. Is that all right?'

Craig nodded.

'Let me know when he arrives.'

Uncle Albert's port-wine nose clashed just as fiercely with his bow-tie, but his fatuous humour was dimmed. Craig thought he looked like some nervous curate calling to offer condolences to a bereaved family. He coughed, patted his wispy hair and hardly knew where to begin.

'Helen, my dear, what awful news,' he said at last. 'I only knew about it when I arrived in London this morning and saw the papers. How are you?'

Helen smiled at him wryly.

'Awfully disturbing business,' Uncle Albert meandered on. He turned to Simone. 'Don't you think so, Miss — er — Mrs. — er — ? You know the extraordinary thing is I didn't know a word about it until I arrived in London. Most extraordinary. But then, as it wasn't in the papers until this morning, one couldn't very well know, could one?' He turned back to Helen Brook. 'Tell me, how are you? Your Aunt suggested I should come up and see you — just a short visit — to know how you were getting on. I had to come up to London anyway to see my stockbroker. He was proposing to buy some shares for me, but I don't think I shall. Not just now. There may be a rise in tin later, they say.' He turned to Craig. 'Are you acquainted with the stock market, Mr. — er — Mr — ?'

Craig shook his head.

'I never seem to have the capital.'

'You're a very fortunate man.' Uncle Albert sighed. 'It really is a most awful nuisance. I hate having to worry about things.' He turned back to Helen. 'Well, my dear, how are you?'

She started to say something, but he went rattling on.

'Of course, my dear, I understand. You must feel most distressed over this terrible calamity. Really, to think that all this should happen since I was down here last. When your poor Aunt reads the papers, she will be most terribly upset.'

Craig went back to his office as the telephone began ringing.

'Mr. Craig?' a girl's voice asked him.

'That's right.'

'Mr. Gabriel Warwick would like to speak to you.'

'I don't mind either,' Craig said, and there was a click as the call was plugged through. Gabriel Warwick's resonant tone came over the wire.

'Good morning, Mr. Craig. Of course, you know what's happened. Dreadful news. I rather wanted to talk to you about it. I wonder if you would be good enough to come along to my office?'

'When?'

'What time could you make it? This morning?'

Craig glanced at his watch.

'Suits me. I'll come right along.'

'I'm very grateful to you, Mr. Craig.'

On his way out Craig told Simone he was going to Gabriel Warwick's office. He said:

'If Marraby calls up, take a message and get on to me pronto.'

She nodded and said:

'Helen's going out to lunch with her uncle.'

Craig paused on his way to the door. He half turned back as if he'd thought of something. Simone looked at him questioningly.

'That is all right?'

Craig hesitated. All he said was:

'Sure.'

He went out.

II

Gabriel Warwick stood up, shook hands with Craig and waved him towards a

316

leather armchair. He pushed a silver cigarette-box across the desk.

'I hope you don't mind my bothering you like this,' he began, 'especially as you were unable to accept my offer to work for me.' He smiled. 'Incidentally, that job's still open if you should change your mind.'

Craig drew at his cigarette. Through a cloud of smoke he murmured:

'Maybe I will when this one folds up on me.'

Gabriel Warwick nodded.

'As you can imagine,' he said, 'I'm more than disturbed by this extraordinary development. I see you're actively engaged on the case for your newspaper.'

'That appears to be the general idea.'

'I'd be glad to have your opinion on the affair. Young Brook is by way of being a friend of mine. I look on him as one of my most promising men. He had every chance of becoming a most valuable executive. If there is a possibility of his being innocent of this dreadful charge, well, as a matter of fact I intend to make myself responsible for his defence. I shall engage the best possible man.'

Craig didn't say anything.

The other went on:

'What I can't understand is why he has not — well — faced the music. A most dangerous thing to do. They're bound to catch him in the end, and then, surely, his behaviour will be held as a strong indication of his guilt.'

'It certainly won't help him.'

The other leant forward a little.

'Have you any possible idea, Craig, where he may be hiding?'

'I know he's in London somewhere. Or was, about half an hour ago.'

'Really? Where was he?'

'My place.'

'Good God! He came to see you?'

'Not exactly.'

'Did he offer any explanation for the way he has acted?'

'Not really. He kind of flashed in and flashed out. So far as I can make out, he just dropped in to tell his wife not to worry.'

'His wife?'

'She dropped in to see me, too. Her

uncle turned up this morning. I'm beginning to feel in the way.'

The other smiled a little. Then he said:

'I suppose you've formed some opinion about this business? I mean, you've probably arrived at some reason why Brook should have murdered these girls? That is if you think he is guilty.'

'I'll tell you,' Craig said. 'I don't think he did strangle them. He knew the first girl all right. He was even in her room at Maida Vale somewhere near the time of the murder. He found her there. But someone else had been there before him. Someone who was afraid she'd open her mouth too much.'

The other's thick eyebrows drew together in a frown.

'Open her mouth too much?'

'It goes like this,' Craig told him. 'Lucy Evans worked in the office of a firm called the South London Property Development Company. She found out about a little racket someone was running. Maybe someone nothing to do with the office. Maybe she just happened to pick up the information. Anyway, whatever it was, she

319

knew about it. Then your Jeffrey Brook meets up with her. She threatens a certain someone who's mixed up with this racket, and who's giving her the run-around, that she'll put in the squeak to Brook. That someone didn't take any chances.'

Craig thought the story sounded good. There was no doubt it had impressed Gabriel Warwick.

'Interesting. Most interesting. And this is the theory you're working on, Craig? When will you have the proof that will clear Jeffrey Brook?'

'Not just yet. There are one or two things need sewing up first.'

Gabriel Warwick tapped with his gold pencil on the desk.

'I'm very grateful to you for coming along,' he said. 'So you think young Brook stands a chance?'

'I think it would help if he'd walk into a police station and explain things.'

The other nodded.

'I imagine the police don't altogether see eye to eye with your theory?'

Craig grinned at him.

'Not altogether. Inspector Marraby has

got a warrant out for him.'

Gabriel Warwick stared at his desk thoughtfully for a moment.

'I wonder if you'd do something for me? Immediately Brook has been arrested, would you let me know? I'd like the chance of giving him my help.'

'I'll do that.'

'Thank you, Mr. Craig.'

III

The midday editions had hit the streets. All of them played up the Jeffrey Brook business for all they were worth.

'SUSPECTED GIRL STRANGLER STILL
AT LARGE
DOUBLE MURDER SUSPECT ELUDES
POLICE
WHERE IS JEFFREY BROOK?'

In milk-bars and restaurants, in omnibuses and tube trains, excitedly masochistic people were made to wonder what it was like to be on the run from the police.

Hunted night and day, afraid to venture out except in disguise, on your guard against everyone, knowing that at any minute an alert eye could have the police at your heels. On the run!

The Jeffrey Brook story conjured up melodramatic mental pictures of a figure skulking in the shadows with fearful backward glances, and peering out warily upon dark streets. Eyes strained for the approach of any uniformed shape that might materialise out of the gloom. Ears taut for following footsteps, the sudden shout of discovery, the rush of pursuers; or the sudden hand on the shoulder.

On the run from the police!

The news editor hurried out of the *Globe* newsroom and turned into the managing editor's office. He slapped down a page-pull on the desk and leant over the other's shoulder as Sullivan began to read:

'SENSATIONAL TURN IN SEARCH FOR MISSING ACCUSED'
'MOTHER OF JEFFREY BROOK TELLS OF HER

'The mother of Jeffrey Brook came into the offices of the *Globe* at three o'clock to-day and gave this newspaper an exclusive statement.

''My son is innocent,' she said. 'I have proof that he did not commit the murder and I shall place it in the proper hands if the police do not withdraw their charge against him. They will not find him. I know where he is, and he is safe.'

'Mrs. Brook is a tall woman of about fifty, with a still beautiful face and greying hair. She was wearing a long grey cloak.

'She informed the *Globe* that she is writing a letter to the Home Secretary to explain the true facts of the case and to demand a withdrawal of the murder charge — '

★　★　★

Sullivan looked up at the news editor.

'It smells from here to Ludgate Circus and back,' he said.

The news editor shrugged.

'That's what the old girl said.'

'Where is she?'

'In the waiting-room. They're going to take some pictures of her right away.'

The internal 'phone on the desk buzzed.

'Yes. When? Where? Okay.' The 'phone was slammed down and Sullivan looked up at the news editor again. 'You've missed your pictures.'

'Eh?'

'She just walked out.'

'Where?'

'They haven't the slightest idea. She just walked out. Apparently she didn't think to leave a message where she was going.'

'The bloody idiots — !'

'All right, all right,' the managing editor calmed the other down. Then, stabbing at the page-pull, he asked: 'Did you check any of this stuff with Craig?'

'No. Why?'

'What's the good of buying a dog and barking yourself? Better get on to him. He may know something.'

He picked up the receiver.

IV

The frosted-glass door opened and Simone came in.

'Mr. Sullivan of the *Globe* on the line. Are you in?'

'Might as well be,' Craig said. 'After all, they're paying me.'

Sullivan read the page-pull to him over the 'phone, adding that the woman in grey had performed a vanishing trick.

'You can't print that junk, anyway,' Craig told the managing editor.

'Why not?'

'Jeffrey Brook's mother would say anything. She's crazy.'

'We're all crazy, more or less.' The managing editor took a broad-minded view of things.

'I mean crazy out of her mind,' Craig said. 'Nuts. Insane.'

'I don't understand. You say she is insane? How do you know?'

Craig smiled a superior smile into the telephone.

'I had it first-hand from her son's wife.'

Sullivan remembered something about

a woman who'd escaped from a mental home in the neighbourhood of Quarry House a few days ago. 'His wife? How did you find her? Where is she?'

'Parked in my flat.'

The other exploded.

'In your flat — ! Why the hell — ?'

'Relax,' Craig told him. 'And keep your newspaper slouches away from my door. Things are going along all right at the moment. Soon as I've got it all nicely tied up for you, I'll dump the story in your office.'

He heard Sullivan draw a deep breath at the other end of the wire.

'Now listen, Craig. You've got a big story — '

'You're telling me it's a big story. Only I know just how big it is. Mrs. Jeffrey Brook is being handled with kid gloves and she's liking it. Relax like I told you.'

'But what are you going to do?'

'Pull in Jeffrey Brook. That's why his wife could turn out to be sort of helpful.'

'All right, then, I'm leaving it to you.'

'You ain't got no choice.'

'But if someone else finds Jeffrey

Brook, or his wife, and we get scooped on this story — '

'You do worry yourself into your grave, don't you?' Craig told him, and rang off. As he lit a cigarette and leaned back in his chair, Simone came in again. Craig eyed her narrowly. She was looking excited about something.

'Someone to see you.'

'I should have my office in the middle of Waterloo Station,' he said through a cloud of cigarette smoke. 'Who?'

'Dolores Brant.'

36

'That one,' Craig said. 'Now maybe we really are getting some place. Just as a matter of interest, have Uncle Albert and niece returned from lunch?'

Simone shook her head.

'They should be back. Perhaps he thought some fresh air would do her good and they've gone for a walk.'

He nodded and took a drag at his cigarette.

'Go ahead and lead in La Brant,' he told her.

As she came into the office the perfume she wore didn't so much trail after her. It just stood up straight alongside and nudged at you. He could see Dolores Brant was in a pretty bad state of nerves. She took the cigarette he gave her, and as he lit it she drew at it quickly so that the glow crept along like a burning fuse.

'Just for the record,' he asked her, 'how did you get my telephone number the other night? Or could it be you just popped up into my secretary's bedroom and found it there?'

She nodded.

'There was an address-book in her suitcase.' Then she was staring at him hard and suddenly asked: 'Do you think this man, Jeffrey Brook, murdered those girls?'

He eyed her for a moment.

'You don't look the morbid type. Why should you be interested in who murdered who?'

Ignoring his question, she went on:

'The police think he did, don't they? The newspapers say so.'

'Newspapers frequently say all sorts of things, but it doesn't necessarily mean they're right.'

Her expression became somewhat distraught.

'Please,' she begged, 'I came to see you because you are a detective and because you know something about this.'

'I sometimes wonder if I do,' he told her.

'You're not sure, then, that this man is the murderer?'

'If it makes life any easier for you, all right, I'm not sure.'

He leaned back and contemplated the tip of his cigarette. He looked up at her and said:

'Why don't you spill it?'

'I wanted to tell the girl that night, but somehow I couldn't. I felt scared. I don't feel so good about it even now.'

'It's up to you,' he told her casually. 'You don't have to say anything to me if you don't feel in the mood. Only thing,' he went on with studied nonchalance, 'if you're worried this Brook character is really in the clear, and you can do something about it, you wouldn't want to have a thing like that on your conscience, would you?'

She bit her red lower lip and then said:

'There's something I ought to tell you. Something that happened to me three days ago. Only if I tell you, you must please keep my name out of it.'

'I wouldn't want to sign a blank cheque for that,' he told her. 'Why don't you quit worrying over yourself and just talk to me? If you've got anything to say, that is.

I'll do what I can to see you don't get hurt.'

'All right,' she said. 'But, you see, I'm scared. I'm the only one who knows. That's what scares me. Being the only one.' She hesitated again and then said: 'How would it be if I told you everything, but left out the man's name?'

He grinned at her bleakly.

'You mean Anthony Webber?'

She drew in her breath in a quick gasp. Her eyes were very wide.

'You know?'

He nodded.

'I know some of it. One thing that interests me a trifle is why you went out of that flat leaving only the walls standing.'

She stubbed out her half-smoked cigarette nervously.

'I used to be very friendly with Tony — Mr Webber.'

'Call him Tony if you want.'

'In fact, we were going to be married. And then I began to realise he was fooling me. He made me the most wonderful promise about helping me with my

331

career. He was going to back me in a big show.' Her mouth twisted into a sour smile. 'I found out he was playing around with some girl in his office. It wasn't that I was jealous, or anything like that. I didn't give a damn. By that time I knew he wasn't going to help me and that his talk had been just talk all along. I told him to go to hell and that I never wanted to see him again.'

Craig supposed that was what he had heard that morning at the offices of the South London Property Development Company. Dolores Brant telling Anthony Webber she was through. He told her to go on.

'Then I read about this girl being murdered. It was a bit of a shock when I realised it was the girl in the office. The girl Tony had been fooling around with. But it wasn't any of my business, and I forgot about it until two or three days later when he came to see me at Tower Court. It was in the afternoon. I thought he'd come to try and make it up with me. He started off by talking that way, saying how he still wanted to help me, back me in a show. And then he said there was something he wanted to ask me. He said I could help him.'

'How? As if I can't guess.

Her eyes flickered at him. She went on:

'He said if anyone were to ask me about him would I swear he was with me from a quarter to eight until nine that Tuesday. The Tuesday before last. Of course, I knew at once why he wanted me to say that. He must have murdered the girl. I was horrified and frightened. I tried not to show I was frightened. I said I'd see him in hell first. I told him to get out.'

She broke off. It was as if she were re-living the scene.

'What happened?'

'I thought he was going to kill me,' she said. Her voice was very low. 'He suddenly seemed to go crazy. He started throwing things about. He knocked me against the wall. I really can't remember what happened. I felt dazed and ill. Then he cleared out. I was scared he would come back again, so I packed up everything and left. I went down to Wittons End — but you know about that.

It was foolish of me, but I was panicky. I thought I'd be safe there. But, of course, I wasn't really. He would have found me again sooner or later. He *had* to find me. He couldn't let me get away, knowing what I did. I felt so helpless and alone. That's why, when your secretary turned up at the Harvest Moon, I thought she was spying for Tony. Then, when I talked to her, I decided she wasn't. I thought she was something to do with the police.'

Craig nodded. The way he had figured it from what Simone had told him had been right.

She was saying:

'I discovered she'd been sent by you, and to me that was as good as the police, so I cleared out. I 'phoned you later so that you wouldn't think it was because I was mixed up with the murders. But this Jeffrey Brook business has been nagging at me and I had to come and see you. Tell you what I knew.'

There was a little silence. Craig thought Dolores Brant had turned in a pretty remarkable testimony. It smashed Anthony Webber's alibi into a lot of very small pieces. He said:

'Did he give you any reason why he wanted you to say he'd been with you during that time?'

'He did,' she said slowly. He admitted going to the girl's — Lucy Evans — house. He said he found her already dead.'

Another one, thought Craig.

Dolores Brant continued:

'He said he knew who killed her, but he wanted me to swear he was with me just in case there were any questions.'

Craig said:

'He said he knew who killed her?'

She nodded.

'He found a man's gold watch and chain in the girl's hand. That's what he said. He said he thought she must have dragged it from the murderer's waistcoat while she was struggling with him.'

A gold watch.

Craig's mind went back to the mysterious visitor who'd butted in on him and Slate Kellett last night at the South London Property Development Company offices. He remembered the man searching the safe and then asking Craig if he'd taken a gold watch.

Maybe Anthony Webber's story could be the truth at that.

An idea began to crystallise at the back of his mind. He was remembering Lucy Evans' letter to Anthony Webber. He was remembering how it mentioned that he was working for somebody else. Somebody higher up. He was thinking, suppose this head boy had been tipped off by Anthony Webber about the Evans girl blackmailing him on account of something she knew? He was thinking, suppose this head boy had bumped off Lucy Evans? Maybe only a few minutes before Jeffrey Brook and Anthony Webber had arrived?

He was talking while he was thinking.

'Did he show you the watch?'

'No. I didn't really believe him. I knew he was just making it up. He didn't fool me. I know Tony too well.'

Maybe you don't know Tony well enough, he was thinking. Craig stood up and walked round the desk to her. He said:

'You've been a great help, Miss Brant.

336

A lot of things are clear to me now that were blurred before you dropped in.'

She put her hand on his arm. He thought her fingers looked like white talons with blood dripping from the ends.

'Does it mean the police will be looking for Tony now?'

'I wouldn't know about that,' he said. 'They may think it an idea to let him roam loose for a while.'

'But why should they do that?'

Her voice got a little shrill.

'In the hope, maybe, he'll lead them to the real murderer.'

She stared at him, her mouth open.

'The real murderer,' she choked. 'But Tony's the murderer. That's why I told you. So the police would get him and keep him away from me.'

'They'll get him before he gets you. Don't you worry.'

'He did it. I know he did it. I've told you the truth. They've got to guard me from him.'

'I've already told you, you're in no danger,' he said. 'Go to an hotel for the next day or two. Any hotel. Forget about

Anthony Webber. And don't go about in a thick veil, either. Unless you deliberately look for him, he won't find you.'

She drew a long, shuddering breath.

'You don't know how scared I am.'

He nodded, eyeing her as he dragged at his cigarette.

'You'll be all right by to-morrow. Within the next few hours this business will be sewn up tight.'

'And they'll have caught Tony?' she queried,

His jaw tightened. He said:

'They'll have the murderer. Supposing we just let it go at that.'

He pressed the bell on his desk and Simone came in.

'Miss Brant is going. She'll be 'phoning later to tell you the hotel where she's staying.'

After Dolores Brant had gone, Craig put a call through to Scotland Yard. As he waited for Marraby to come on the line, he wondered idly if Dolores Brant was at that moment telephoning Anthony Webber. He didn't give much for the thought, but you never could tell with women.

37

I

Craig told Inspector Marraby:

'In case you care, I've just gone and had Anthony Webber's alibi blown sky-high. All the same, I have to admit I don't think he did it.'

He heard the triumphant tone in the other's voice.

'You mean it's Jeffrey Brook after all?'

'You're too quick,' Craig said. 'I don't mean that, either.' He gave him the story Dolores Brant had left behind with the last lingering memory of her perfume. At the end of it, he added, 'By the way, did you know Brook's mother recently tottered into the *Globe* office, told them she knew where Sonny was and tottered out again without saying good-bye or where she was going?'

'His mother?'

'I wouldn't let yourself get worked up

over it. She's crazy. Escaped from a mental home, near where Jeffrey Brook lives.'

'All the same, can't we get hold of her. Where is she now?'

'I told you. She's done a disappearing trick.'

'We can pick her up. What does she look like?'

Craig gave Marraby the description the *Globe* had passed on to him. Woman aged about fifty, tall, wearing grey cloak.

'That's something for my bloodhounds to work on,' the Inspector said. 'We should be able to nose her out. About this Brant woman, perhaps a chat with her wouldn't do any harm either.'

'I'll 'phone you back as soon as she lets me know her hotel,' Craig promised him.

'Fine.'

'And remember,' Craig said, 'I'm playing ball with you like I expect you to play ball with me. The moment you pinch Jeffrey Brook, you tip me.'

'A policeman's word,' Marraby said sententiously, 'is his bond.'

'It had better be this time,' Craig said somewhat jeeringly, and rang off. He looked up as Simone came in from the outer office. 'Who now?'

'You will never guess,' she said.

Craig's gaze shifted past her shoulder and he said, bleakly:

'The Professor.'

'How did you — ?' Simone began and then turned as the familiar decrepit figure edged past her, nursing his bowler hat.

'Good afternoon,' the Professor beamed. 'Good afternoon.'

Craig caught the reddish glint behind the dark spectacles.

'I'm very busy,' he said bluntly.

'I, too, have been extremely busy,' was the bland reply, and Craig threw Simone a bitter look as she closed the door behind her.

'I have discovered something of most vital importance,' the Professor went on.

'If it's another chart — ?'

'Not exactly. Though I have, of course, been pursuing my investigations along those lines which I brought to your notice at our last meeting. In fact, I have now completed the murderer's horoscope, basing my calculations on the data we discussed then. Do you remember?'

Craig said he remembered.

'Those calculations were fully confirmed by the second murder which occurred that same evening. This, of course, was extremely gratifying for me, though,' he went on, 'not so gratifying for the victim concerned.'

Craig agreed that the victim concerned probably hadn't felt so happy about it.

'When I heard over the radio the news of that second unfortunate girl's death, I telephoned you, to point out how it fitted in with the calculations arrived at on my chart. You were, however, not at home.'

'Too bad.'

The Professor hugged his bowler hat to him more tightly. Craig perceived he was about to make one of his pronouncements. The other spoke slowly and with dark significance.

'I have discovered,' he said, 'that this is a very fatal day.'

'Who for? You or me?'

'My dear sir, I am speaking extremely seriously. I have to inform you that this is a particularly fatal day for the murderer. It is written in the stars that he will strike again.'

The Professor paused impressively.

'Someone in London,' he went on, 'will die tonight by the same pair of hands that strangled the other two.'

Craig said, levelly:

'Listen, pal. I'm going to give you some advice. Life is short. We're all going to be dead before long, which means you as well. So why don't you get wise to yourself and let up throwing your star-tangled spanners into the works. If you're really burning up to do something helpful around the place, I'll tell you what you can do. You can snoop around London and try and find a tall old woman, dressed in grey, for me.'

The Professor didn't appear to take any offence. Neither did his expression betray chagrin or disappointment. He asked, placidly:

'Woman in grey? Who is she?'

'Jeffrey Brook's mother.'

'And you mean you want to find her?' Craig nodded.

'That's putting it mild.'

The Professor scratched his bald dome reflectively.

'Yes,' he said. 'Yes. I think I know where she is.'

'What!'

'I have seen this elderly person in grey. She is staying at a small hotel next door to where I live in Bloomsbury. She arrived yesterday, as I recall. I remember the grey cloak she was wearing. Her appearance was rather conspicuous.'

'What's the name of this hotel?'

'It's called the Moreland Private Hotel. In Moreland Street, just off Gordon Square.'

Craig picked up the receiver and got through to Inspector Marraby again.

II

Craig's taxi swung into Moreland Street just behind a police car. They drew up simultaneously outside the Moreland Private Hotel.

Craig paid off the taxi and waited for Inspector Marraby to lever himself out of the police car. With the Inspector was his sergeant.

'You think Jeffrey Brook may be here as well?' Craig shrugged.

'I wouldn't know. Old Mother Hubbard said she knows where he is, which may be true, even if she is crackers.'

'Come on,' the Inspector said.

The Moreland Private Hotel was a narrow, seedy-looking establishment, hardly more than a boarding-house. Over the fanlight was the name with some of the letters missing. The front door was open and they crowded into the dingy hall. A red-faced woman, wearing a pince-nez and rustling black, came forward. She was the proprietress, she said.

Marraby announced who he was and asked if a Mrs. Brook was staying there.

'Her name's Broadhurst,' Craig reminded him, 'but she's probably given a phoney name anyhow.'

There was a sudden exclamation from

behind them. It was the sergeant, who had hung back, and was taking a look up and down the street.

'What's the matter?'

'A woman in grey,' the sergeant said. 'Coming along now.'

The Inspector dived into the street. Craig followed him. The woman was approaching them only a few yards away. She stopped as she saw them and stood there, her gaze wandering from them to the police car and back again. She must have realised at once this meant the end of her freedom. With a quick movement that sent her grey cape swirling, she turned and hurried off in the direction from which she'd come. Her walk quickened into a run.

'After her,' Marraby snapped and followed the sergeant.

The woman heard their footsteps and turned blindly to cross the road. There was a squeal of brakes as a car swung round a corner, swerving to avoid her. But it failed to make it. A mudguard caught a corner of the flowing grey cape and dragged her under the wheels.

III

Craig and Inspector Marraby paced up and down the corridor outside the hospital casualty ward. They stopped as a nurse came out and Marraby spoke to her quickly.

'She's still unconscious,' the nurse told him.

'When do you think she'll be able to talk?'

The nurse looked doubtful.

'It's a cervical fracture and she's lost a lot of blood.'

'You mean she's going to die?'

'I don't know.'

'D'you think she may come round just for a few minutes. Enough to answer one or two questions?'

'The doctor is giving her oxygen now. If she regains consciousness I'll let you know, of course.'

'Thanks. We'll wait.'

The nurse went back to the door and they resumed their pacing up and down the corridor. Craig lit a cigarette, but Marraby wouldn't take one from him.

'Damn the woman,' he grumbled morosely. He sounded as if the woman had deliberately engineered the accident. 'Why the hell don't people look where they're going?'

The minutes went by. Craig was about to light a fresh cigarette from his stub when the door opened again. It was the nurse, followed by the house surgeon.

'How is she?' Marraby queried.

The house surgeon shook his head.

'I'm afraid it's all over,' he said.

38

The house in West Street was as silent and dim as it had been on his previous visit. The damp, musty smell still clung to the place.

Craig had decided this was to be the next move in the routine and had managed to duck Marraby after they left the hospital. He climbed the stairs, his footsteps echoing on the bare, creaky boards. He reached the top flat and stuck his thumb against the bell.

The door was opened by the woman with the too-brassy hair whom he had presumed was Mrs. Alfred Vincent. Her eyes were pale blue and sharp and suspicious. She held the door only half-open.

'What do you want?'

'I don't think you know me, but I have a little proposition which might interest you and your husband.'

She stared at him, then down at his

foot, which he had slid forward strategically so she couldn't close the door. Her face was dark with distrust.

'It's about a Mr. Webber,' Craig murmured. 'Anthony Webber.'

She drew in her breath with a sudden gasp.

'We don't know any Mr. Webber,' she said.

Craig shrugged.

'In that case,' he said casually, 'maybe I'll take my little proposition to the police.'

Her knuckles showed white against the door. Her mouth was working. Then she gulped and said, in a low voice:

'I'll tell my husband.'

The door closed behind him and he followed her along the little hall.

'Who is it?'

It was Vincent's resonant voice calling from the sitting-room.

'Someone to see you,' she called back, a note of warning in her voice. 'A — a friend of Tony's.'

'I'm not sure he would agree to that,' Craig murmured as he stood behind the woman in the doorway.

The man got up from his chair. His grey face seemed to sag with fear. His hands crumpled the newspaper he'd been reading in a convulsive movement.

'Who are you?'

'Sit down,' Craig told him amiably. He turned to the woman. 'You can relax, too, if you want.'

She crossed over to him and stood beside him as if to bolster up his courage.

Craig lit a cigarette.

'Now let's be grown-up,' he said, through a cloud of cigarette-smoke. 'Don't let's waste time pretending we don't know what I'm talking about. I'm wise to your racket. See? I know you pick up a nice fat cheque every time you start up one of your cosy little fires. You've been doing it for quite a long time now and you must have made, shall we say, eight thousand, three hundred and twenty?'

A sound that could have been a moan escaped Vincent's lips. The woman's grip on his shoulder tightened.

'All right,' Craig said. 'We'll settle for

eight thousand, three hundred and twenty.'

'We haven't the faintest idea what you're talking about,' the woman said through her teeth. 'Get out of here. Get out.'

Craig said to the man:

'What do you think, Alfred? Shall I pop along and spill all this to you know who?'

The man tried to say something, but all that happened was that strangled moan again.

Craig nodded understandingly.

'I thought *you* would want to be reasonable.'

The woman was speaking again, but Craig cut her short.

'You're doing your best, but it won't get you, or him, anywhere at all. You see,' and his voice was suddenly rasping, 'I know about you and you know I know, and I know you know I know.' He spoke to the man again. 'How would you like to clear out of here pronto and start up that garage?'

Vincent found his voice.

'How — how did you know about that?'

'I've got X-ray eyes,' Craig told him pleasantly.

The man looked at him, his eyes like a whipped dog's. He patted his wife's hand.

'Perhaps we had better listen to him, my dear.'

She didn't answer. She just stared at Craig stonily, the corners of her mouth turned down bitterly.

Craig took a long drag at his cigarette and said:

'It's no personal grudge I've got against you. I don't mind very much if you have sent a lot of valuable property up in smoke. It isn't my property, so you wouldn't expect me to burst into tears. I am what you might call impartial. Detached. Just a private dick trying to get along and keep my nose clean. I don't want to push anyone around. Even if they try to push me around, I'd sooner keep out of their way than shove back. And I'm different from the ordinary cops in this way, also. I can sometimes sit on the fence and let people go by. People like you, for instance. I can let you go by and it won't worry me at all. Provided you answer a couple of questions first. You can go down and open up that garage and never give me another thought. You'd like that, wouldn't you?'

The woman's expression had relaxed a little A little colour had come into Vincent's skin. A gleam of something that might have been hope showed at the back of his eyes.

Craig tapped the ash off his cigarette.

'Let's say we begin with the name of the head boy,' he said. 'The man at the top who pays you. The boss of this racket. Let's kick-off with that, for a start.'

There was no answer.

Craig's eyes became chips of flint.

'I had the impression we understood each other,' he drawled. 'Don't tell me I made a mistake. Don't say you aren't going to play. Or maybe you didn't hear me properly the first time. So I'll make it easier to grasp. Is your boss Anthony Webber or not? If not, who?'

'You mean,' the man said slowly, 'you won't go to the police?'

'I can't give it you in shorter words than I've been using.'

'All right.'

Vincent looked up at his wife and then back at Craig. He licked his lips. 'I'll tell you everything I know. But I don't know who is the head man. It was Tony who started me off. I've always had my instructions from him. But there's somebody else, only I don't know who he is. I swear I don't.'

Craig's reaction didn't give away his faint sense of disappointment. Somehow he'd felt he was on to something. That he was about to dig out of the Vincents the identity of the fire-bug-in-chief and murderer of Lucy Evans and Rita Spear.

'So you got your instructions from Anthony Webber?' he asked. 'So that's all you know? Webber's boss is all wrapped round in a cloud of mystery. That's what you want me to believe?'

'It's true. We don't know who he is.'

It was the brassy blonde, her face thrust forward in emphasis.

Craig eyed her face. As faces went, he didn't care for it much, but he knew, right at this moment, there was truth behind it.

He told her: 'I'm not accusing, just

asking you. If you say you don't know the name of the boss, I'll settle for that. One thing you might know the answer to. Anthony Webber had another blaze lined up for you two or three days ago and then he called it off. What was this dump he had in mind for you to put a light to?'

'It was a warehouse in Thamesway Street. Excelsior Fur Company warehouse. That is, if they do any more,' he went on. 'Tony was scared over something the last time he 'phoned. Perhaps they'll drop the whole business now.'

Craig decided he'd got all he could. From the door, he said:

'Take my tip and move out while the moving's good. This racket is coming unstuck.'

'You'll stand by your promise — ?' Vincent started to say.

'We went into all that. I told you it's the man at the top I'm aiming for.'

He went down into the street and found a taxi.

Back at his office, Craig called the *Globe*. Might be something had come in about Jeffrey Brook, a tip-off from some unexpected source that he could chase. But there was only the usual junk.

Like: Woman in Streatham had 'phoned through to say a man was hiding underneath her bed. He had been there all day and wouldn't come out and she was positive he was Jeffrey Brook.

Or: Woman in Highgate had started screeching over the wire there was a man in her linen-cupboard who answered to the wanted man's description. She got to using peculiar, not to say highly improper language before the desk hung up on her.

Several goons in widely separated London districts had managed to spot Jeffrey Brook practically simultaneously. He had been spotted at the Zoo, outside a Golders Green cinema, at the Elephant and Castle, at Houndsditch and in Camden Town.

Just another slab of garbled and false information a newspaper is accustomed to sorting out every day.

Simone said Marraby had not come through. Craig hoped he wasn't trying any funny stuff and holding out on him. He persuaded himself to give Marraby the benefit of the doubt and wasn't quite sure if he should feel happy the cops hadn't picked up Jeffrey Brook, or worried that Brook, still at large, might get the chance of fulfilling his threat to fix a certain someone.

Simone told him Dolores Brant had 'phoned giving the hotel where she was staying. It was a name Craig had never heard of and was obviously some obscure side-street dump Euston way. It looked like Dolores Brant really had got Anthony Webber on her mind. Craig grinned to himself at the thought of that shapely parcel of glamour scared away in some dreary bedroom and climbing up the wall with fright every time she heard anyone pass her door. He told Simone to pass the address on to Marraby who'd probably put a man on to watch the place, just in case.

He glanced at his watch.

'Uncle Albert and the girl come back?'

Simone shook her head.

'They're taking quite a walk,' he said.

She looked at him suddenly. She said:

'You do not think anything has

happened to them?'

'No, I don't think anything's happened to them,' he said slowly. 'Though, come to think, it could. I was wondering?'

'What?'

'I should get a statement from Helen Brook. On paper and signed. Her story about her husband, leading up to the vanishing trick.'

'You mean for the *Globe?*'

Craig nodded.

'She'd be doing it for Jeffrey Brook. It would be a kind of public vindication. She could leave out the — shall we call it white blackmail business.' He grinned bleakly. 'That mightn't help. But the rest of it would look all right. It would come in handy when we pinched the real murderer and the case against Jeffrey Brook falls to pieces.'

Simone nodded. She looked up suddenly and said:

'That sounds like someone, now. It will be Helen and her uncle.'

'Tell her I'd like to talk to her. Ward off Uncle Albert. He sort of gets in my hair.'

She smiled at him.

'I know. But he means very well.'

'Not well enough to keep his trap shut,' he threw after her as she went out.

She came back in a moment with Helen Brook. There was more colour in the girl's face. She looked less haggard. The fresh air had perked her up. She said:

'Uncle Albert didn't come back with me.'

Craig shot her a quick look.

'What's the matter? He get lost?'

She shook her head and smiled a little.

'We were passing a cinema. It was some film he'd read about a lot, but it hadn't come his way. He asked me if I would like to see it, but I told him no, I thought I'd come back. The film was just starting, so I told him it was all right, I didn't mind, and he popped in. It was — a murder film,' she added, her voice low. 'It had a gruesome title.'

Craig glanced at Simone.

'I think I'll be getting along.' He nodded towards Helen Brook. 'Tell her what I told you, and get her talking. You could have it all ready for me by the time I get back.'

Helen Brook looked at him and he told her: 'A little thing you could do to help your husband. Simone'll explain.'

Simone smiled at her. She asked him:

'If Marraby or anybody 'phones, what do I say?'

'Say I've gone to look for somebody. Somebody who'll talk and say something at the same time.'

39

With a little grin of satisfaction, Anthony Webber stood up from locking the new rawhide suitcase. He glanced around the softly-lit bedroom of his flat at the rest of his luggage, smiling to himself at the labels. Paris. He was going a hell of a long way farther than Paris!

He crossed to the dressing-table mirror to straighten his tie which was a little awry. He lit a cigarette and smoked it for a moment. He moved casually over to the creamy coloured telephone. A slight hesitation, then he lifted the receiver. Presently the familiar voice sounded in his ears. He said, his tone quietly confident:

'This is Webber. Have you the money ready? Five thousand. In cash. Yes. I have the watch. Where do we meet? Very well. I'll be there in half an hour.'

He cradled the receiver with an expression of thoughtful satisfaction. He drew at his cigarette and went over to the dressing-table again. From it he took up a gold watch and broken chain and slipped them into his pocket.

The telephone burr-burred quietly.

'It's the hall porter, sir. Your taxi's here.'

Anthony Webber glanced at his wrist-watch and told the man to come up and collect the luggage. A few minutes later he was telling the taxi-driver to take him to Victoria Station. He wanted to go on from there to another address, he said.

Craig's taxi arrived just in time for him to see Anthony Webber get in and his taxi drive off. He caught a glimpse of the luggage. So the bird was on the wing. He was getting out while the going was good.

'Keep on the tail of the taxi in front,' he told his driver.

'Wot? You mean like on the pictures, mate?'

'If it's more fun for you that way,' Craig told him, and they shot off.

At Victoria Station, Craig told his driver to pull up some way behind Anthony Webber. As he got out, he saw

Webber walking away with the porter and his luggage. He hadn't paid off his taxi. Was he dumping his stuff and then going on somewhere else? Craig told his driver to wait.

After a few moments, Anthony Webber reappeared, hurried into his taxi and it drove off. Craig kept him in view along Victoria Street and the Strand and Fleet Street. Past Blackfriars, and then a turning down towards the waterfront.

As the streets grew more deserted, Craig told his driver to hang back. He didn't want Anthony Webber to suspect anyone was on his tail. They nearly lost him once or twice, but they managed to hang on. It was growing dark and a mist was beginning to creep up from the river. Then they were in Thamesway Street, his driver said, as the taxi ahead stopped.

'Don't pull up. Keep on moving.'

'Okay.'

Craig saw Anthony Webber get out and, with a word to his driver, walk quickly along the dimly-lit street. Suddenly he disappeared through high wooden gates. Craig waited till they could turn a corner before he stopped his taxi. Telling the driver to stick around, he went quickly back and paused outside the gates through which Anthony Webber had vanished.

The note from a tug's siren quivered on the air and died away. Above the slightly open door cut in the wide gate, Craig could make out:

Excelsior Fur Company.

He found himself in a cobble-stoned yard. At the end he could glimpse the gaunt outlines of a derrick silhouetted against the stars. The river slapped against the stone wharf. On his right, the warehouse made a great dark mass.

Cautiously he moved across and found a narrow doorway. He stepped inside. It was as dark as the inside of a tar barrel. He waited until his eyes began to accustom themselves to the gloom. The faint light from a window helped him to make out that he was in an office. Facing him an open door made a black rectangle. He moved like a shadow towards it.

Suddenly he caught the sound of voices.

They came from somewhere overhead. He was in a large room and just ahead of him a faint glow showed through a trap-door. Wooden steps led up to it. He paused momentarily at the foot of the steps. They were men's voices — two men speaking. He began to climb quietly. His eyes reached the edge of the trap-door.

A few yards away Anthony Webber was talking in a low voice. He had his back to Craig and was masking the other man. An electric bulb threw a pool of harsh light over them. The pool didn't reach the trap-door, so that Craig was in comparative darkness. Anthony Webber was saying:

'You've brought the money in cash?'

'Let's see first if you're keeping your part of the bargain,' came the other voice.

With a sharp sense of shock, Craig realised who it was. Anthony Webber moved, and Craig could now see the other figure more clearly. It was the same man who'd appeared in the office of the South London Property Development Company last night to interupt him and Slate Kellett. The way he stood, with his hat over his eyes and his overcoat collar turned up.

Craig stared at him. The head man. The big boy himself.

He'd played it very smoothly, he admitted to himself wryly. As the shock wore off, he began to realise just how smoothly. Who the hell would have suspected *him*? And yet, now it all crowded back on him, Craig could see how it fitted in like a jig-saw. He'd been a bright boy, all right. The way he'd strung *him* along, too, Craig was thinking, had been nice. His mind went back to when they'd met and he saw how the smart so-and-so's approach had deliberately edged him off his track. The line of gab he'd used. Put it over like an actor. A superb actor handling the lines with just the right touch. And then Craig remembered the hint of a hunch he'd had about him. Or was he just kidding himself now? He smiled bleakly.

'Why this sudden distrust?' Anthony Webber was saying.

The light glinted on the watch he drew from his pocket.

'I was just wondering if you might have forgotten,' the other said, a hint of amusement in his tone. Then, in a sudden vicious movement, he swung his walking-stick and brought the heavy top of it down on Webber's head with terrific force.

Anthony Webber sagged at the knees. The other deftly caught the watch as he struck again. Anthony Webber folded up to pitch forward flat on his face. With a glance at the inert figure, the other moved out of the pool of light. A match flared. Craig saw the man bend over a heap of wooden shavings, then draw back as they burst into flame.

The smartness of it flashed through Craig's mind. The way the other had dealt with Anthony Webber. He was going to burn the one man who'd known he was fire-bug-in-chief and murderer of Lucy Evans and Rita Spear. He'd been too cunning to shoot his blackmailer. The charred skeleton might be discovered later, the bullet found. His way would be much safer. Almost detection-proof.

The figure turned, moved towards the

trap-door, his shadow dancing fantastically on the wall as the flames, leaping higher, spread towards the body. His sudden movement caught Craig unawares. Though he ducked his head quickly, he heard the other's exclamation and swift rush towards him. Craig slid down the steps, but the man above flung himself recklessly through the trap-door and fell upon him.

Craig was knocked backwards by the other's weight. He felt a sickening blow on the side of his head. His adversary was beating at him with his stick. Craig drove his fist upwards and drew from the other a gasp of pain. But the stick kept beating at him. It was then Craig realised he was in for a brawl with a raving maniac.

The flames above were spreading like fiery quicksilver, crackling and hissing. Already they were consuming the far wall. Already the edge of the trap-door was alight. And now, behind the crackling of burning wood, sounded the increasing roar of a furnace as the draught fanned the fire. Soon the entire building would be a holocaust.

Craig got one hand underneath the other's jaw and forced his head backwards, driving his other fist into the body above him with every ounce of his strength. They were both gasping and choked by the smoke that swirled round them. The man was dribbling saliva and mouthing obscenities, and though the blows of the stick were wilder and feebler, their culminating effect had already told on Craig. One more bash and he knew he'd go under.

He hooked again into the other's belly as the stick lifted once more. But the blow never fell. The stick was suddenly wrenched away and someone was dragging the other backwards.

Craig pulled himself to his knees, sobbing for breath, and saw against the smoke and flames who the newcomer was. Jeffrey Brook. With the stick he had grabbed, he was beating hysterically at the struggling figure. The figure collapsed, but Jeffrey Brook didn't let up bashing him.

'You'll kill him!' Craig managed to yell. 'Bloody fool! We've got to get him out of here — alive.'

He lurched forward and, snatching the stick from Jeffrey Brook, grabbed the other man's collar.

'Come on. Give me a hand,' he grunted. 'Don't you see, we've got to turn him over to the cops instead of you?'

Jeffrey Brook seemed to catch on.

'Yes — yes,' he muttered, and together they lugged Gabriel Warwick out into the yard.

It was hopeless to go back for Anthony Webber. The upper part of the warehouse was a roaring inferno.

Suddenly people were pushing into the yard, shouting excitedly. A fire-engine sounded in the distance, clanging nearer and nearer. Craig leant against Jeffrey Brook for support. He nodded at Gabriel Warwick heaped at their feet.

He said, hoarsely:

'Damn near carried out your threat.'

Jeffrey Brook said:

'I waited outside the offices — had to risk police spotting me — and followed him. I meant to scare him into confessing he'd killed those two girls if it was the last thing I did. To me it stuck out a mile he

371

must have done. And I was going to threaten him I'd kill him if he wouldn't talk. Near here, I lost him. Then I saw the fire.'

There were more fire-engines racing nearer. More people were milling around, their faces flickering reddish-yellow. A couple of policemen were pushing through the mob towards them. Jeffrey Brook was suddenly peering into Craig's face.

'You all right?'

Craig started to grin at him, but it hurt too much.

'You must have taken a hell of a beating from the swine,' Jeffrey Brook went on.

Craig said, his mouth twisted with pain:

'If it's one thing you have to be to be a private dick, you have to be tough.'

The bells of the fire-engines were suddenly louder. Jeffrey Brook's face started going away from him. Then it was back, close and enormous, his eyes wide with anxiety. He was saying something Craig couldn't hear, the noise of the fire-bells was so loud inside his head. For a flash he had a picture of the blazing warehouse, the mob's faces, weird in the reflected glow, the two cops approaching. It stood out, clear and distinct. He thought Jeffrey Brook was asking him again if he were all right. He wished he would speak louder.

'Honest, I feel fine,' he heard himself say.

Then it was as if somebody dropped a black curtain before his eyes, and he passed out in a dead faint.

THE END

We do hope that you have enjoyed reading this large print book.

Did you know that all of our titles are available for purchase?

We publish a wide range of high quality large print books including:
Romances, Mysteries, Classics
General Fiction
Non Fiction and Westerns

Special interest titles available in large print are:
The Little Oxford Dictionary
Music Book, Song Book
Hymn Book, Service Book

Also available from us courtesy of Oxford University Press:
Young Readers' Dictionary
(large print edition)
Young Readers' Thesaurus
(large print edition)

For further information or a free brochure, please contact us at:
Ulverscroft Large Print Books Ltd.,
The Green, Bradgate Road, Anstey,
Leicester, LE7 7FU, England.
Tel: (00 44) **0116 236 4325**
Fax: (00 44) **0116 234 0205**

A TIME FOR MURDER

John Glasby

Carlos Galecci, a top man in organized crime, has been murdered — and the manner of his death is extraordinary . . . He'd last been seen the previous night, entering his private vault, to which only he knew the combination. When he fails to emerge by the next morning, his staff have the metal door cut open — to discover Galecci dead with a knife in his back. Private detective Johnny Merak is hired to find the murderer and discover how the impossible crime was committed — but is soon under threat of death himself . . .

THE MASTER MUST DIE

John Russell Fearn

Gyron de London, a powerful industrialist of the year 2190, receives a letter warning him of his doom on the 30th March, three weeks hence. Despite his precautions — being sealed in a guarded, radiation-proof cube — he dies on the specified day, as forecast! When scientific investigator Adam Quirke is called to investigate, he discovers that de London had been the victim of a highly scientific murder — but who was the murderer, and how was this apparently impossible crime committed?